DECEIVED

REGINALD BUCHANAN

author of *The Killer Postman* and *Writer's Block*

outskirts press

Deceived

v3.0

This is a work of fiction. The events and characters described herein are imaginary and are not intended to refer to specific places or living persons. The opinions expressed in this manuscript are solely the opinions of the author and do not represent the opinions or thoughts of the publisher. The author has represented and warranted full ownership and/or legal right to publish all the materials in this book.

Outskirts Press, Inc.
http://www.outskirtspress.com

ISBN: 978-1-4327-9830-7

Library of Congress Control Number: 2017913239

PRINTED IN THE UNITED STATES OF AMERICA

This book is dedicated to my angel, best friend and loving wife ... Cheri Buchanan. Our family and friends miss and love you tremendously. Rest in peace.

1

Right after volleyball practice Joan Witherspoon ran toward the school bus and climbed aboard with the rest of the female varsity volleyball members. Joan had no interest in playing volleyball, during her first two years of high school, but that all changed after she became a senior. Every chance she got, Joan would watch the female volleyball players from various countries play competitive volleyball on TV. Also, watching the women interact in the USA Volleyball Tournament really boosted her interest. Joan had fallen in love with volleyball ... so she joined her school's volleyball team.

Joan was a natural at every sport that she'd ever participated in. She excelled in softball, lacrosse, and basketball, but her favorite sport was volleyball. She was selected to play on the volleyball team because of her power when hitting the ball and her great blocking techniques. Her position as middle hitter required good footwork, shoulder flexibility, strength, and endurance. She had all of those great athletic qualities and was genuinely adored by her teammates, friends, family, and community.

The bus driver, Henry, and their coach, Walter, waited for the girls to be seated before driving off. After starting the engine, Henry activated the windshield wipers because it had just started to rain. The sun had set, and the weather had taken a turn for the worse on this ninth day of March 2000. The temperature had dropped from fifty degrees to a bone-chilling thirty degrees. It was a quarter to six when Henry started pulling away from the school—the rain had started to fall a little harder.

Walter had promised to treat the girls to dinner at Jason's Malt Shop because he knew practice would run late. He made sure to let their parents know not to expect them back for dinner and that he was providing their kids with a late meal for the evening.

Seven-minutes later, they all arrived at Jason's Malt Shop. After having their hamburgers, fries, and milk shakes, the girls hustled back onto the bus, thanked Walter, and took their seats. Henry started the bus, pulled out of Jason's Malt Shop parking lot, and drove off. Henry dropped off his first passenger shortly after leaving the malt shop at a quarter to seven.

Halfway home, Joan started to think about her figure 8 puffer fish. She was upset with herself because she had forgotten to feed them before she left for school that morning. Joan knew her fish were starving, but she was powerless to do anything about it now. At first, she wanted Henry to speed it up a bit, but she changed her mind and wanted Henry to drive cautiously after seeing how bad the weather and road conditions were. Her poor fish would have to wait a few more minutes before being fed.

Joan's parents, Bill and Rachel, had bought her ten figure 8 puffer fish and a hundred-gallon fish tank two months before at a pet shop in Durham, North Carolina, for her eighteenth birthday. They had the fish and fish tank delivered to their home via UPS. They wanted to buy her a cat, but Joan insisted that taking care of ten fish would be much easier than caring for a cat.

Bill and Rachel were both forty-five-years-old when Joan, their only child, was born. They were classic examples of how some people looked and lived during the 1970s. Bill had lengthy graying hair with long sideburns. He loved wearing tie-dyed shirts and peace symbols. Rachel had long blonde hair and wore ratty jeans, tie-dyed blouses, and multicolored love beads. They were a modest couple who had never owned a car, a computer, or cell phones. Bill and Rachel had preferred to utilize a typewriter versus a computer. Also, their land-line, at their home, was much better than some cancer causing cell phone. They never worried about emergencies when they were away from home because of the phone booths located throughout their town. Most importantly, they never needed the use of an automobile, because of the community's public bus system. That bus system took them back and forth to work every day, as well as to all the other businesses and social gatherings in their town of Fall City, South Carolina.

They both worked at the only library Fall City had. Rachel stored and retrieved books and ordered magazines and newspapers as one of two female librarians who worked there. She loved assisting customers with the checking out and in of various library items. She also took the time, twice a week, to hold her own reading sessions for the young children of Fall City. Rachel would have the parents bring along their kids every Friday and Saturday afternoon to the library to hear various stories. The adults and kids loved hearing Rachel read stories by Dr. Seuss and Beatrix Potter. Rachel was treasured by everyone.

Bill was the conservation and library preservation technician. He repaired, reattached, and cleaned all the books. He realized that the care and repair of books played an increasingly vital part in their library and community. The two elementary schools and only high school really appreciated his dedication to the upkeep of their books. Every other month, Bill would hold a book conservation class at the library. He would demonstrate how to repair, clean, tape, and glue books to preserve them. His classes consisted of mainly children, a few adults, and a handful of high school students.

If life seemed simple and uncomplicated for Bill and Rachel, it wasn't. Dr. Wilborn, the town physician, had advised them over and over again to stop their chain smoking, but they conveniently ignored him. He begged them to drive to Durham with him to get complete physicals, but they refused. They just kept on smoking as Dr. Wilborn watched their health decline.

Joan was one of the first girls to be dropped off at home. She said good-bye to her teammates and stepped off of the bus. She started to walk toward her house but caught a fleeting glimpse of Edith coming toward her out the corner of her eye. Edith was a very active seventy-year-old friend of Joan and her parents. Edith was on her bike, riding recklessly toward Joan at a high rate of speed, not realizing that she was on a collision course with Joan. At the last second, just before impact, Joan quickly maneuvered out of Edith's way preventing Edith from running her over.

"Be careful, Edith! It's too dark out here for you to be riding your bike around. You might hurt yourself or someone else," Joan yelled out.

Edith turned back, looked at Joan, and shouted, "Sorry, I didn't see you, Joan. Thank God I didn't hit you. I'm on my way home now. I'll be more careful."

Edith had taken her eyes off the road for a moment as she turned to respond to Joan, and she almost rode her bike into the six-foot-long gully alongside the road. Luckily for her, she swerved her bike away from the gully at the last second; otherwise she would have fallen face-first, bike and all, into that four-foot-deep water-filled gully. Joan watched Edith as she continued to pedal her bike down the road toward the lake and disappear into the darkness.

"That was close. Thank goodness Edith is going home," Joan said.

Joan's thoughts went back to her fish, and she started running through her front yard toward her front porch through the ankle-high wet grass. As she ran ... the force of the rain was so strong that Joan had to cover her face with her hands. She shivered as the cold, wet rain circumvented her coat and shirt and made contact with her skin.

She ran onto her porch and wiped her face clear of the rain with her hands. She reached into her sweatpants pocket and removed her house key to open her front door, but the door was unlocked. Her door being unlocked was odd, but she didn't pay much attention to that because she was more preoccupied with the feeding of her fish.

It was seven o'clock when she opened her front door, entered, turned on the living room light, and looked in the direction of her fish tank. Her fish were all stationary and resting on the bed of her tank.

Henry blew his horn after seeing Joan enter her home, and then he drove off. Joan waved good bye to Henry, Walter, and the rest of her friends as the bus disappeared down the dark gravel road. Joan heard the loud beeping of the bus's horn before she closed her front door.

"That Edith probably rode her bike right into the path of the bus and Henry had to blow his horn to alert her. He may even had to veer his bus out of her way. Poor Edith hasn't been quite right since her eighty-one-year-old husband died in his sleep a couple of years ago," Joan said.

Right after closing her front door ... In a firm but somewhat loud voice, Joan shouted out, "Mom, Dad ... I'm home!"

There was an eerie silence in the house, which puzzled her for a moment. She thought it was strange that all the lights were out in the house at seven o'clock in the evening, but she soon forgot about that after going into the kitchen, turning the light on, and removing the container of fish food from one of the kitchen cabinets. She placed the food on the kitchen table, removed her wet coat, and slung it over one of the kitchen chairs before grabbing the food and dashing back into the living room to feed her fish.

She removed the cover to the fish tank and started singing the song "Spinning Wheel" by Blood, Sweat & Tears to her fish. She was told, a few weeks ago, that puffer fish loved to be sung to, so she started singing to them. Her ten figure 8 puffer fish had football-shaped bodies, large heads, big protruding eyes, dark-gray colored upper bodies and white colored underbellies. They were all about six inches in length. Her puffer fish swam toward the top of the tank after hearing a few lines of the song, and Joan smiled and started pouring in portions of the food. After distributing their food, Joan went back into the kitchen, where she placed her fish food back into the cabinet. She paused for a moment to think about next Friday's volleyball game against Pawtucket High School. They had to beat Pawtucket or be eliminated from the playoffs. This was a grudge match, in a sense, because Pawtucket had beaten Joan and her teammates in three out of five matches a month ago. Not only had Pawtucket beaten them, but they had bloodied a couple of the girls' noses after spiking the ball directly into their faces. Joan and her teammates were angry and ready for such a rematch.

Joan removed an apple from the refrigerator, rubbed it on her shirt, bit into the apple, and walked into the living room. She picked up the remote control for her TV and sat down on the couch. Before clicking on the TV, she looked over at her beautiful puffer fish and watched them gleefully swimming around after eating their food.

She cut on the TV, threw both her legs up onto the coffee table and started surfing the channels for something to watch. After an exhaustive ten-minute search, she gave up and turned the TV off. She glanced over at her fish again and smiled, knowing that they were full, but her thoughts suddenly went back to her parents. She assumed that they were probably upstairs, or at Albert and Mary's house next door playing cards or gossiping about someone or something. But she didn't remember seeing any lights on at Albert and Mary's home when she got off of the bus.

Joan took another bite of her apple and glanced at her watch—it was seven-twenty-five. There weren't any notes for her on the kitchen table or on top of the TV set.

"If they had left the house, they would have left me a note," Joan said after removing her legs from atop the coffee table. She looked at the fish tank and then looked over at the stairway leading upstairs.

She stood up, placed her half-eaten apple on top of the coffee table along with the remote control, and started walking in the direction of the stairs. Halfway to the stairs, she stopped, looked toward the second floor, and yelled out, "Mom ... Dad." But no one replied.

She made her way to the foot of the stairs and then quickly made her way to the second floor. She noticed that her parent's bedroom door was ajar, and it sounded as if the TV was on. She walked toward the door, peeped in, and saw that her mom was lying on the bed and her dad was sitting in his leather reclining chair. They both were watching TV.

Joan had spoken with her parents just before leaving for school that morning at six o'clock. They had told her to have a good day at school and said they would see her when she'd returned home.

"Mom, dad," Joan quietly whispered as if she were afraid to disturb them, but they ignored her; they didn't budge.

Joan used the glare from their TV to navigate the room after entering. She didn't want to turn on the light for fear of troubling them.

Joan noticed that her mother's cup was tipped over on the floor alongside a broken plate with a small portion of food on it. It was as if she'd just dropped them on the floor from where she lay. It wasn't like her mother to do that. Also, a pack of cigarettes was open and lying on the floor next to the plate. Joan quickly looked over at her dad, who was steadily looking at the TV from his recliner. It was an odd sight because her dad was clutching his cup with one hand, while his other hand was clasping his shirt near his heart. The ashtray on the arm of the recliner was full of cigarette butts. He too had a plate of half-eaten food on the floor near his feet, but his plate wasn't broken.

"Mom, Dad," Joan said, louder this time. But they still didn't move.

Joan walked over to the bed, grabbed her mother's bare foot, and shook it, but her mother didn't respond. Her mother's foot was as cold as a block of ice, but Joan continued to shake it in a fit of panic.

"Mom ... WAKE UP!" Joan shouted.

Joan moved closer to her mother, knelt down in front of her, and looked into her hollow black eyes. Her mother's face was pale and haggard. Snot had hardened underneath her nose, and a gooey black substance had oozed out from her mouth, covering her lips.

Joan stood up, gasped in horror, and moved toward her father. Her dad's eyes were blood red, and his mouth was wide open. His face was contorted and strained. It looked as if every blood vessel in his forehead had tripled in size.

"Oh my God," Joan shrieked just before picking up the phone to dial 911.

2

Sheriff Mike McClotin, Deputy Phil Goony, and Dr. Kenneth Wilborn all arrived at Joan's home twenty-minutes after Ruth, the acting 911 operator and secretary for the sheriff, received Joan's frantic call for help.

Joan's front door was wide open, so the sheriff, Dr. Wilborn, and Deputy Goony rushed right in and found Joan standing motionless in the middle of the living room floor.

The sheriff rushed right up to her and said, "Joan, are you okay? Are your parents okay?"

Joan didn't utter a word; she just glowered at the sheriff.

During Sheriff McClotin's twenty-five year tenure, as the sheriff for Fall City, South Carolina, he had maintained stability by delving into citizens' complaints, investigating traffic accidents, resolving disputes, arresting drunks and suspects involved in petty crimes, thwarting bar fights, ticketing speeders, and performing as a justice of the peace and a makeshift judge. He was the kind of sheriff that took care of his staff, close friends, and most importantly—the community. Sheriff

McClotin was an unmarried fifty-six-year-old robust man about five feet eleven, weighing 240 pounds, with a signature crew cut hairstyle.

The sheriff wrapped his arms around Joan, and said, "Everything is going to be fine. Don't you worry."

The sheriff guided her over to the couch and forced her to sit down where he removed his hat and sat down next to her.

"Where are your parents?" Dr. Wilborn asked.

"They're upstairs ... upstairs in ... in ... their bedroom. I think they ... they ... are dead," Joan responded.

Dr. Kenneth Wilborn was the only physician that this small town of 1,955 people had had for the past thirty-one years. He was in his late sixties, stood six feet tall, and had a small, rickety body. His short graying hair was progressively falling out from front to back, and he had a rat's nest of a moustache. He was the physician, the paramedic, the psychiatrist, and the priest all wrapped up into one. Dr. Wilborn knew what to do for colds, the flu, infections, cuts, bruises, broken limbs, pregnancies, and mild illnesses, but any serious illnesses or injuries were referred to the adjoining county. That adjoining county was one hundred miles away, and it was Durham, North Carolina.

Deputy Phil Goony looked in the direction of the stairs, adjusted his tie, straightened his gig line, and started walking toward the stairs which lead to the second floor. Dr. Wilborn, holding on to his black bag, followed Deputy Goony up the stairs while the sheriff continued to comfort Joan.

The weirdest feeling came over the sheriff as he continued to console Joan. Joan's outwardly emotions revealed nothing in the way of shock or dismay about her parents' deaths—if her parents were truly dead. She wasn't trembling, nervous, or agitated in the least possible way. Something was peculiar, and he sensed it. Over the years, Sheriff McClotin had become familiar with people's reactions and behaviors in relation to certain situations. Being in the presence of grieving individuals for so many years had made him more attuned to their sorrows. Sheriff McClotin had a good sense, or at least he thought, for how people often felt or reacted after someone close to them were injured or had died. Witnessing children, teenagers, young adults, and elderly people completely lose it upon hearing about or observing the death of their love ones made him more compassionate and caring. Those individuals, who witnessed their loved ones' demise went into shock, fainted, wept, paced back and forth, had nervous breakdowns, or had to be given a sedative to prevent them from having a nervous breakdown. He had seen numerous other reactions from individuals who had lost loved ones, but nothing like Joan's. For some reason, he thought Joan was reacting in an odd way. Joan hadn't shed a tear since he and the others had arrived. She was the very first citizen of Fall City that Sheriff McClotin could remember who hadn't shed a tear after losing a family member to a natural death, medical crisis, or serious injury. It seemed unusual that a young girl who proclaimed to love her parents so much could be so calm. To believe that her parents' were dead ... and act in this way was odd.

Upon entering the bedroom, Dr. Wilborn's and Deputy Goony's facial expressions changed from bad to worse as they gazed upon the bodies of their friends. Dr. Wilborn checked for vital signs, but there were none. After checking for any signs of life, Dr. Wilborn examined the foamy black substance on Bill's and Rachel's lips. He immediately thought that their constant smoking had finally caught up with them. That black fluid on their lips, he felt, had probably made its way up from their diseased lungs and out through their mouths. Dr. Wilborn had on many occasions observed Bill and Rachel cough up black phlegm when he was in their company. They would put their hands to their mouths in the middle of their conversation, stop talking, and leave to spit out the phlegm that had accumulated in their mouths. Dr. Wilborn had insisted that they see a specialist in Durham, but they seem to always refuse.

Deputy Goony removed a digital camera from his back pocket and began taking pictures of the bedroom and corpses. After taking a number of pictures, he placed the camera back into his pocket, removed a pair of latex gloves from his shirt pocket, and started to examine the bodies. He gently searched their scalps and looked over their torsos, arms, legs, and necks for any sign of physical violence. He was in search of cuts, wounds, or blunt trauma, but he found nothing related to any type of bodily harm—not even a trace of blood.

Deputy Phil Goony was a twenty-seven-year-old bachelor who was born and raised in Fall City. He was a gaunt fellow who weighed about 160 pounds. He stood six feet even and wore his hair down to his shoulders, but he had a receding hairline that made him look much older than his age. After graduating high school he applied for the deputy position working for Sheriff McClotin and was hired. Deputy Goony had been working for Sheriff McClotin for seven years now. He was one of two deputies working for the sheriff. Deputy Goony had seniority over the other deputy by three years and was counted on the most by Sheriff McClotin to get things accomplished.

Dr. Wilborn was shocked at the expression on Bill's face. His face was so contorted and strained that the doctor felt he must have died of a heart attack. His last act must have been painful, because he was clutching his chest in the area of his heart. Rachel's face was insipid, and her eyes were wide open—more so than Bill's eyes. It seemed as though Rachel had spewed out more of that gooey black substance from her mouth than Bill had.

After Deputy Goony filled out his death scene checklist, Dr. Wilborn pronounced the causes of death for both Bill and Rachel to be apparent heart attacks. The contributing factors to their heart attacks were chronic bronchitis caused from cigarette smoking, and poor health. The visual proof of bronchitis was the black mucus hardened to their lips, which had been uprooted from their lungs after their many years of chain smoking. Knowing Bill and Rachel's medical background made it much easier for him to come to that conclusion. Dr. Wilborn had knowledge of Bill and Rachel's history of heavy smoking for years, but he had never fully explained to Joan what harm the cigarette smoking was doing to her parents' bodies. He'd never informed Joan about the trip he and her parents had taken concerning their health. Last year Dr. Wilborn had accompanied Bill and Rachel to see Dr. Reynolds in Durham, North Carolina, when he detected their coughing spells and phlegm problems were starting to get worse. In addition to this, Dr. Wilborn noticed increases in their heart rates and blood pressure after many of their coughing spells. This worried Dr. Wilborn, so he finally convinced them to see Dr. Reynolds. Dr. Wilborn had consulted with Dr. Reynolds about Bill's and Rachel's medical histories prior to them leaving for Durham.

Dr. Reynolds's blood tests, chest X-rays, and thorough medical exams of Bill and Rachel revealed that they both had coronary heart disease. The fatty buildup in their arteries was preventing the appropriate amount of blood flow to their heart muscles. Also, Bill and Rachel had smoker's cough and chronic bronchitis.

Dr. Reynolds wanted to schedule a pulmonary function test to see how well their lungs were working, but Bill and Rachel refused. After four hours of various testing, they both had had enough for one day and wanted to return to Fall City.

Dr. Wilborn was disappointed with both of them for refusing to complete all of the tests, but he'd known them for many years and was aware that both of them were as stubborn as bulls.

Dr. Reynolds prescribed them both Theophylline and Lipitor. The Theophylline he prescribed was used to prevent coughing, wheezing, shortness of breath, and bronchitis. Lipitor was used, aside from other uses, to reduce the risk of heart attack and stroke.

Dr. Reynolds explained to Bill and Rachel that they could have a heart attack if they didn't take the prescribed medications. He also insisted that they stop smoking, and eat healthier foods. Bill and Rachel thanked Dr. Reynolds and ensured him that they would take the medications and quit smoking. Dr. Reynolds's shook Bill and Rachel's hand and thanked them for their cooperation. He also thanked Dr. Wilborn for bringing them in for a checkup. Five minutes later Dr. Wilborn, Bill and Rachel were driving back to Fall City. Both Bill and Rachel immediately lit up a cigarette as soon as they were out of eyesight of Dr. Reynolds. Dr. Wilborn just frowned and shook his head in disagreement as Bill and Rachel puffed away.

Deputy Goony and Dr. Wilborn made their way back down the stairs to confirm what Joan had feared—that her parents were dead. Dr. Wilborn walked over to Joan, who was still sitting down and being comforted by the sheriff, looked into her eyes and said, "Joan, I don't know any other way to say this, but both of your parents have passed away."

Joan quickly looked at the sheriff and then Deputy Goony but didn't say a word. She just lowered her head and gazed at the floor.

Dr. Wilborn knelt down beside her, pulled out a handkerchief from his black bag, wiped the perspiration from her forehead, and then felt her forehead and cheeks with the palm of his hand. Her face wasn't cold or clammy; nor was it pale. Dr. Wilborn thought that Joan was in shock, but she wasn't. He took hold of her right wrist and listened to her heart rate. Her heart rate was in the normal range, and she didn't have any of the classic symptoms associated with shock. The doctor believed that Joan was in some sort of despair ... maybe even denial.

Dr. Wilborn stood up and said, "Sheriff, can I talk to you in private?"

"Sure thing, Doc," the sheriff responded.

"Let's go into the kitchen," Dr. Wilborn said.

Deputy Goony pushed his hat back so it would ride a little higher on his forehead and said, "Sheriff, before you go ... nothing out of the ordinary was found up there. Most importantly, there were no signs of any foul play whatsoever. It looked as though they may have died from some sort of preexisting medical complications. The doc will tell you more about it."

"Good job, deputy. Just stay here with Joan while I talk to Dr. Wilborn," the sheriff said.

"Not a problem," Deputy Goony responded.

The sheriff tried to stand up to follow Dr. Wilborn into the kitchen, but Joan grabbed his hand and held on tight to prevent him from leaving.

"Joan, I know you're confused and hurt right now, but I have to talk to Dr. Wilborn for a minute. I'll be right back. But in the meantime, Deputy Goony will be here to look after you." The sheriff gently pulled his hand free of Joan's grip, stood up, and walked toward the kitchen.

Deputy Goony immediately sat down next to Joan after the sheriff and Dr. Wilborn entered the kitchen. Deputy Goony placed his arm over her shoulders to comfort her.

"What's going on, Doc?" the sheriff said after entering the kitchen.

Dr. Wilborn placed his black bag on top of the kitchen table, took a seat, and said, "Nothing to be alarmed about, but I wanted to let you know my findings before you climb those stairs and do your investigation."

Sheriff McClotin leaned up against the refrigerator, folded his arms across his chest, and said, "Deputy Goony said that they died of some sort of medical complications. It won't be much of an investigation on my part if they died of medical complications. No need for me to even look over their bodies if there wasn't any foul play involved. The last thing I want to do is climb those stairs and look at the corpses of my two friends. Doc, I'll be in agreement with anything you say about the cause of their deaths."

"I have determined that they died of heart attacks caused by their pulmonary problems—chronic bronchitis. Dr. Reynolds warned me that Bill and Rachel could end up like this ... and they did. An autopsy won't be required. I'll fill out the death certificates and turn the bodies over to Joan and assist her with the proper burial arrangements."

"Sounds good to me," the sheriff said. "We don't need to drag this thing out because of the condition Joan is in right now. The sooner we bury them, the better for Joan."

"Agreed. As of today, our small community of 1,955 people has just been reduced to 1,953. Sheriff, I don't know how you and your two deputies manage to keep the peace around here. We have been virtually crime free."

"It isn't that bad. Thank God we've never had any real catastrophes, because I don't know how our one hospital with only thirty-two beds, a small morgue, two nurses, and yourself would be able to handle such emergencies. Doc, I guess all you have to do now is contact Joey, our mortician."

"I'll give him a call as soon as we are done here. We are lucky that there haven't been any major accidents, illnesses, or deaths for years. Especially involving large numbers of people. The last natural deaths we had were a few years ago. It was Edith's husband Mel ... he died in his sleep. And, Gregg ... he died while working at his gas station with his son ... just fell right out while sweeping up his garage from a blood clot. I believe both were in their eighties. Otherwise, than that, no other deaths to report. Oh, I almost forgot to tell you. A few years ago I had a lawyer from Durham assist Bill and Rachel in filling out a will. Bill and Rachel wanted everything to go as smoothly as possible for Joan after their deaths. They stated in their will that Joan would be the executor of their estate and Albert and Mary Niphon would be trustees. Thank God that Albert and Mary befriended Bill and Rachel. Things will go smoothly for Joan thanks to that will."

"It's a good thing that Albert and Mary lives right next door to Bill and Rachel. They'll be right there for Joan at a moment's notice for whatever assistance she may need after this horrible tragedy. Well, I guess we had better get back out there to Joan."

"Go ahead ... I'll be right with you," Dr. Wilborn replied.

The sheriff left the kitchen while Dr. Wilborn sat motionless at the kitchen table and wondered about Joan: *She seemed indifferent to everything that was happening. No signs of any deep, outward remorse for the sudden and unexpected death of her parents. Maybe she was in another state of mind? I've never witnessed an individual who had just lost loved ones act this way. It's uncharacteristic. Maybe it's some other form of despair that she might have fallen into that I'm not aware of.*

Dr. Wilborn stood up, grabbed his black bag, and walked back into the living room to tend to Joan.

3

Besides Sheriff McClotin and Dr. Wilborn, Joan had no one else to confide in after her parents' untimely deaths, except for her next-door neighbors Albert and Mary Niphon. Dr. Wilborn and the sheriff were a big help in the beginning, but Albert and Mary started caring more for Joan after the death of her parents, which freed up Dr. Wilborn and the sheriff to carry on with their regular duties. Joan's parents were buried just four days before Joan and her volleyball teammates played Pawtucket to decide who went to the playoffs. Some people were shocked to see Joan participate in the volleyball games so soon after her parent's deaths, but many brushed it off as a way for her to divert her attention away from such sorrow. Joan's team beat Pawtucket, and Joan enacted some personal payback herself by intentionally spiking the ball into the face of one of the Pawtucket players and breaking her nose. Although Joan's team moved on to the playoffs, they lost in the first round and were eliminated. They took the loss hard but were happy that they had beaten Pawtucket to get to the playoffs.

After losing in the playoffs, Joan and the other girls piled onto their school bus to be driven home. Regardless of their having been eliminated in the first round of the playoffs, everyone seemed to be in good spirits.

Henry dropped Joan off at her home and waited for Joan to enter before he pulled away. Once Joan stepped into her home, she felt a wave of uneasiness and isolation come over her. Living all alone was too much to take. She immediately sat down on her couch and contemplated what to do next. She knew that she had to leave the loneliness and sadness that surrounded her. Joan decided that she wanted to move out of her parents' home. She wanted to get away from that house as soon as possible.

The following morning, Joan asked Albert and Mary if she could move in with them. Without hesitation, Albert and Mary both said yes. But there was one problem; Joan wanted to know, before moving in, if there was room for her puffer fish. Albert and Mary had no problem with that scenario and moved Joan and her puffer fish into their home that same day. Besides, they had promised Bill and Rachel that they would take care of Joan if anything ever happened to them.

Albert and Mary didn't have any children, so they directed all their love and attention toward Joan. Joan was just like a daughter to them. Eventually they put Joan's parents' home up for sale and sold it during Joan's senior year in high school. Joan attended Duke University in Durham,

North Carolina, after she graduated from high school. Albert and Mary assisted Joan by using a portion of the money made from selling Bill and Rachel's home to buy Joan a brand-new Volvo to make the 210-mile round-trip commute between their home and Duke University.

Albert and Mary had sold Bill and Rachel's home to Marcus Pollard. Marcus was a rich landowner who had numerous homes in Fall City and Durham. His plan was to renovate the two-story home in six-years or less and put it up for sale again. Until then, the house would receive the proper maintenance and upkeep on a periodic basis, but it would stay unoccupied.

While in college, Joan stayed on campus during the week and returned home every weekend to be with Albert and Mary. It was a relief for Joan to know that her fish were being properly cared for while she was away at college.

Although Joan's major in college was criminology, her passion and interest seemed to be acting. She felt a sense of relaxation and calm when she participated in her drama classes. Joan volunteered to play various roles in many different plays at Duke University, and she enjoyed every minute of it.

Since her sophomore year at Duke, she wanted to go to Baltimore just to enroll at the nationally famous Buchanan Acting School. She had read about the great acting opportunities at this school and wanted to move to Baltimore after graduating from Duke. She envisioned using her criminology degree to work in the Baltimore Police Department while she attended the Buchanan Acting School.

Joan didn't start to get serious about having a boyfriend until her senior year in college. And it was during her senior year of college that she started to have problems with the opposite sex. It seemed as though every man she met treated her badly, had a girlfriend, was married, or was gay. Romance wasn't in the cards for Joan, even though she was gorgeous in her own right. She weighed 120 pounds and stood five feet ten inches tall. She had an attractive full-figured body; long, curly black hair; hazel eyes; and a tactful, ladylike personality. And to top everything off, everyone loved her. Joan took her courting seriously because she really wanted to find a husband and eventually get married.

In her zeal to get married, Joan almost married a nerd by the name of Jerry MaGillicutty. Jerry worked at one of the Best Buy stores in Durham. This wasn't just any nerd; he was a Geek Squad nerd who worked in the computer department of Best Buy. She met Jerry after bringing her laptop to Best Buy to have it repaired. Fortunately for her, Jerry was the technician on duty, and he repaired her laptop for free even after she insisted on paying for the repair. She thanked him for fixing her laptop and invited him to join her for lunch sometime. Jerry accepted the invitation, and that's how the romance started.

Jerry was a dark-haired, freckle-faced man

who weighed 110 pounds soaking wet. He stood five feet six inches tall and could have passed for an eighteen-year-old with his boyish looks, but he was actually twenty-five-years-old—just three years older than Joan. For some strange reason, she felt an attraction to Jerry. He was known as Jerry the geek around town and wasn't very sociable, but he was brilliant when it came to repairing computers. He could repair any computer no matter what the problem was. He won Joan over by often taking her out to dinner and showering her with flowers, candy, and free software for her laptop. Unfortunately, this love affair abruptly ended just as fast as it had started.

Joan awoke one morning after two months of dating Jerry and took a long, hard look at the picture of him positioned on her nightstand. At that very moment, Joan noticed, for the first time, that Jerry had rosacea. It covered a portion of his nose and cheeks. It was bad enough that Jerry had freckles too. Also she noticed that his nose was a little askew. Jerry was smiling in the photograph, and it really revealed his crooked and stained teeth. Even his bifocals were sitting unevenly across the bridge of his nose. All of a sudden, Jerry started looking like some type of animal to her. He resembled a weasel that wore glasses. Joan cursed herself for thinking badly of Jerry, but his picture had hit a nerve with her.

Joan had been lonely for love when she first met Jerry. At the time, his physical features didn't bother her. She either didn't really notice those features or she just completely ignored them. Either way, she had fallen madly in love with Jerry MaGillicutty.

Jerry was polite, gentlemanly, and courteous. And most importantly, he listened. All the other men just wanted one thing from Joan, and that one thing was sex. She had loved Jerry for his personality, kindness, sincerity, and honesty, but now she just didn't want to be romantically involved with him anymore because of his facial features.

All in all, Joan had to make a decision about Jerry. She really did like him, but she didn't love him anymore, so she broke off the relationship. Jerry the geek was devastated, but he eventually got over it. It took six long months for him to get through the pain of losing Joan. Jerry almost lost his job during the first few months after their breakup because he couldn't concentrate on his work. During those months, Joan was always on his mind. Jerry was on the verge of having a nervous breakdown. He even contemplated quitting his job, but he finally sought counseling to save his job and his sanity. After counseling and therapy, he became his old self again. He became that smart, ingenious, goofy-acting geek that everyone loved—except for Joan. He threw himself back into fixing computers at the same level he had been at prior to meeting Joan. His whole life was dedicated to his work once again, and Joan was a thing of the past. Jerry "the geek" MaGillicutty went back to business as usual, and Joan continued to search for that perfect man.

4

Albert and Mary noticed how Joan's behavior started to change during her senior year of college. At first they thought nothing of Joan's odd ways and behavior, but Mary became worried when she saw Joan burn all of her parents' photos. Mary had watched Joan carry the framed pictures out to their backyard, dig a small hole in the ground and place them in it, spray lighter fluid onto them, and then set them ablaze. It all happened late one evening when Joan crept out from her bedroom and quietly tiptoed out to the backyard, via the kitchen, to destroy the photos. Joan had no idea that Mary had been awakened by the sound of the kitchen door being opened. Mary quickly left her bedroom and went into the kitchen to investigate. Mary looked out her kitchen window and into the backyard, where she saw Joan burning her parents' pictures—frames and all. Mary hastily returned to her bedroom before Joan completed her dastardly task, without Joan ever noticing. Mary confirmed this dreadful event when she searched Joan's room the following morning and discovered that all of her parents' pictures were gone.

Mary even dug up the scorched picture frames and ashes after Joan had left the house the next day. Mary placed the remains of the picture frames and ashes back where she found them, covered them up, and informed Albert.

Mary and Albert were both shocked to discover that Joan had burned a gold-filled locket containing her parents' pictures, as well as an antique gold Victorian multipicture frame that held photos of her with her parents. Both of those items combined were worth about $400. Albert and Mary were stunned and confused; they didn't know what to do. They also noticed that Joan never talked about her parents after their deaths; nor did she visit their graves after they were buried. It seemed as if Joan wanted nothing more to do with her parents after they'd died.

Albert and Mary never had any problems with Joan while she lived with them, until she burned her parents' pictures. They didn't know what to do or whom to talk to about Joan's peculiar behavior. Sadly, they both started to suspect that Joan may have had something to do with the demise of her parents. The only person they could share this with was Dr. Wilborn. After a couple of days of debating whether to notify Dr. Wilborn about Joan's behavior, they eventually did.

5

"Have a seat," Dr. Wilborn said to Albert and Mary after they entered his office.

They both took a seat on the couch, which was facing Dr. Wilborn's desk. Dr. Wilborn's office was small, and he didn't have a nurse or secretary to assist him.

Behind Dr. Wilborn's desk, hanging on the wall, was a large framed poster of the Hippocratic Oath. His degree from the University of Alabama School of Medicine was framed and hanging on the wall over his watercooler, which was right next to his restroom. His refrigerator, near the back door exit, had a couple of four-inch-tall doctor dolls, carrying black bags, sitting atop it. His desk was free of clutter. He had a telephone, phone book, legal pad, and his black doctor's bag all spaced out evenly on top of his desk.

Dr. Wilborn leaned back in his chair and said, "Okay ... so what's the problem with Joan?"

Albert scooted forward on the couch, wrung his hands, and said, "We think Joan has been acting very strange lately."

"Very strange," Mary repeated.

Dr. Wilborn leaned forward, placed his elbows on his desk, and said, "Strange ... in what way?"

Albert and Mary looked at each other with guilty expressions and immediately wanted to leave, but they didn't. Albert cleared his throat to respond to the question, but Mary beat him to it.

"Dr. Wilborn ... you know Albert and I love Joan with all our hearts."

"Yes I know," Dr. Wilborn replied.

"We've taken care of her as if she were our own child," Mary continued.

"I realize that," Dr. Wilborn said.

"There isn't anything in the world we wouldn't do for Joan," Albert said.

At that point, Dr. Wilborn raised his arms in the air and said, "Mary ... Albert—please get to the point. I know you two have taken care of Joan for almost four years and have given her the best upbringing a person would ever want, so cut to the chase and tell me what's bothering you two!"

Without hesitation Mary quickly blurted out, "We think Joan murdered her parents."

Dr. Wilborn's eyebrows shot up in surprise, and his eyes widened with alarm before he said, "Wait one minute. Her parents died about four years ago of heart disease related to smoking. You can't possibly sit here and tell me that Joan murdered her parents. What evidence do you have that proves she murdered her parents?"

Albert's body tensed up, and his eyes moved toward Mary. He quickly looked at Dr. Wilborn and said, "We don't have any evidence, but—"

Dr. Wilborn interrupted Albert before he could finish. "I thought not. So why do you think she killed her parents?"

Mary cleared her throat, paused, and said, "We may not have any evidence that implicates Joan, but I watched her burn her parents' pictures, and she refuses to visit her parents' grave site. Albert and I have visited that grave site at least eight times since they've died, but Joan has gone only once ... and that was the day they were buried. I've even asked her to pick out flowers to place on their graves from time-to-time, but she refuses to do so."

"She only sold her parents' house to get rid of their memories," Albert said. "She didn't want to keep anything that reminded her of her parents."

"Okay, so Joan wanted to rid herself of her parents' home and belongings. Is there anything wrong with a person wanting to rid themselves of anything that reminded them of their parents' horrible deaths? Seeing her parents' pictures and other items that belonged to them probably made her sad. So what if she sold her home and burned some pictures. Come on, guys! I've seen people who've lost their loved ones do stranger things than that. You know as well as I that Joan seemed to be in another state of mind after her parents died. That's why I prescribed her Zoloft ... she's attending college now and seems to be leading a productive life. That medicine helped her to get through that whole ordeal."

"Dr. Wilborn, in order to understand her

bizarre actions, you would have to have observed Joan as we have been doing these past few months," Albert said.

"What is going on here?" Dr. Wilborn asked.

Albert looked over at Mary and said, "Go ahead and tell the doctor the rest of the story."

"Doctor ... you don't know the half of it. Joan was an angel during the first three years after the death of her parents, but this year, her fourth year with us, she turned into something evil. Some nights we could hear Joan crying and asking God for forgiveness. Her bedroom is right next to ours, and we could hear her voice radiating through the wall. On average Joan cries out loudly a couple times a week, and it's always late at night. Her crying out loud for forgiveness from God wakes us up every time. It has got so bad that we had to knock on her bedroom door a few times to see what was going on ... to see if we could help her. But, every time when we knocked on her door, the crying and begging mysteriously stopped. When Joan opened her door, she wasn't crying or upset; she looked normal. We were puzzled and amazed at how fast all the racket had stopped. We asked her if everything was okay and she simply said yes. We tried to explain to her that we heard her crying and asking God to forgive her, but she looked at us as if we were crazy. She told us that she wasn't crying or talking to God. She said we must be hearing things. After our conversation ended, Joan said good night and then slammed her door shut. This type of confrontation occurred a number of times between Joan and us. After a while, I began to wonder if we were crazy—if we were hearing things. Albert and I talked it over and came to the conclusion that we weren't hearing things. We believed that Joan was actually doing these things."

The doctor rubbed his chin and said, "Are you two sure you weren't hearing things? Sometimes you might hear the wind howling, or some wild animal making a sound, and think it's something else."

"There were no howling winds or any animals making any noise," Albert said. "We actually heard Joan crying out loud during her conversations with God. We tried to talk to her about it, but she always denied it. We actually lost sleep over this. We didn't want to tell anyone about this, because it would have been a betrayal of trust—a trust we had built with Joan. Besides, the crying and conversations with God lessened as the past few months went on, and everything almost went back to normal."

The doctor shifted nervously in his chair and said, "Almost went back to normal?"

"Yes ... almost. Although Joan stopped her midnight talks with God ... her behavior became a little weirder," Mary said.

"Much weirder," Albert added. "A whole week went by and we didn't hear a sound come out of Joan's bedroom. We thought that she was fine, but she had become depressed and withdrawn. She even started to have delusions."

"Delusions? What kind of delusions?" Dr. Wilborn asked.

Albert frowned, rubbed the back of his neck, took in a deep breath, exhaled, and said, "Joan told us that one Friday evening she was abducted by aliens on her drive back from Duke University. She said that a spaceship with very bright lights hovered over her car and caused it to completely stop. Joan said she tried to start her car again, but it wouldn't work. After a few more seconds of unsuccessfully trying to start her car, she opened her car door and got out. She looked up toward the bright lights hovering over her car, and then she passed out. When she awoke, it was Saturday morning and she was sitting in her car at the exact same spot where it had stalled the night before, with her hands on the steering wheel. Confused and frightened, she started her car and drove straight home. She only remembers being subjected to various experiments performed by those aliens. She never elaborated on those experiments ... even after we pleaded with her."

"I can't believe Joan would make up something like that ... being abducted by aliens," Dr. Wilborn said. "Do you think her abduction by these aliens might have been a delusion?"

"Of course," Mary said.

Dr. Wilborn stood up, walked around to the front of his desk, took a seat on the top of it, and said, "I'll have a talk with her about this. If she's really having these delusions, I believe I can provide her with the proper medical help, but I'm still confused about one thing."

"What's that?" Albert asked.

Dr. Wilborn returned to his chair and sat down. "Why do you two think she murdered her parents?"

Mary started to cry. She wiped a tear from her cheek and said, "We just have a hunch that she has done something evil. It just feels that way. I hate to say this, but sometimes when Joan is around ... I get the creeps. Besides, Joan has never displayed any remorse after her parents' death. We think she's asking God for his forgiveness because she murdered them. You should have heard some of the conversations she had with God. Joan was crying as she begged God to forgive her for the terrible sins that she'd committed. I can't really explain it, but deep in my heart I believe she murdered her parents."

"I know this all sounds crazy, but you would need to have heard and seen the things Joan did to understand the situation," Albert said.

Dr. Wilborn thought back to that night Joan's parents died. He remembered how Joan had shown no remorse. He opened his desk drawer, grabbed his bottle of Tylenol, removed two pills, and walked over to the watercooler. After filling up one of the paper cups with water, he placed the pills into his mouth, drank the water, and sat back down at his desk. "Okay. This is what I'm going to do. I'll call her in and talk with her about this whole matter. It may not be Joan's fault. She could be having a negative reaction to the Zoloft I prescribed to her."

"Doctor, there is no medicine on this planet

that would make you act the way Joan has been acting," Mary said.

"I'm not totally sure about that. I'll probably have to change her medication if she is really having these problems."

"We can't thank you enough for looking into this," Albert said. "Please don't think we are bad people. We really want to help Joan. We wouldn't have come to you if we didn't believe you could help her."

"Don't worry about a thing. I'll have her back to normal in no time, but I still don't believe Joan would murder her parents. Besides, her parents died from numerous medical complications that led up to their fatal heart attacks."

"That's what you think! We think otherwise, but please don't tell Joan that we think she murdered her parents," Mary said.

"You won't have to worry about me repeating that to her," Dr. Wilborn said.

"We appreciate that," Albert replied.

Albert and Mary stood up, thanked Dr. Wilborn, and left.

Dr. Wilborn was mystified. He rubbed his forehead and thought about how he was going to approach Joan about all of this.

6

For the next couple of days, Albert and Mary felt guilty about what they had divulged to Dr. Wilborn, but they knew it was for the good of Joan. They could hardly look Joan in her eyes when they talked to her after disclosing that information to Dr. Wilborn. They also cut their conversations short and distanced themselves from her as much as possible because they felt ashamed. Joan thought something was peculiar about their behavior, but she ignored it because she was excited and looking forward to graduating from Duke University in the next couple of months.

Dr. Wilborn had not yet talked to Joan about her conversations with God, or her alien abduction, but Albert and Mary knew he would be calling her soon—and that's when things would get interesting.

7

"Joan, I want to thank you for dropping by. I won't keep you long. Please have a seat," Dr. Wilborn said after giving her a hug.

"I hope this isn't anything serious," Joan replied as she sat down on the couch.

Joan looked confused and really didn't know why Dr. Wilborn had called her two days ago and asked her to stop by. After Joan took a seat, she became a little nervous, not knowing what Dr. Wilborn wanted to talk to her about. All types of things raced through Joan's mind as she adjusted her position on the couch to feel a little more comfortable: *Maybe Dr. Wilborn found something wrong with my blood. I had my blood taken after having a complete physical performed about three weeks ago. Is he going to tell me that I have cancer or something?*

Dr. Wilborn sat down, placed his elbows on top of his desk, lowered his head, and then ran his fingers through his thinning hair. He then leaned back into his chair, placed his hands into the pockets of his three-quarter-length white smock and said, "By the way, your blood work came back from Durham, and everything is fine ... you passed your physical."

Joan let out a sigh of relief. "Thank goodness. I thought you called me here to tell me that I had some type of incurable disease."

"No ... it's not that at all. You're a healthy young woman. But there is something I need to ask you about. This may sound a bit foolish, but ... did you ever get abducted by aliens?"

Joan's eyes widened in disbelief. She laughed nervously and said, "Are you kidding me? Aliens? I've never been abducted by aliens in my life. That's crazy! Is that what you wanted to talk to me about?"

Dr. Wilborn, feeling a little embarrassed, removed his hands from his pockets, folded his arms across his chest, and said, "Yes, and the fact that you supposedly asked God for forgiveness a number of times in a very loud tone—so loud that you woke up Albert and Mary."

Joan felt as if a ton of bricks had just been dropped on top of her head. All the wind was suddenly sucked out of her lungs, and she was ready to faint.

"Dr. Wilborn, everything that you just mentioned is a lie. I've prayed before, but not so loud as to wake Albert and Mary. Did Albert and Mary tell you these things?"

"I hate to say this, but yes."

"Why would Albert and Mary make up such stories? That doesn't make any sense."

Dr. Wilborn stood up, walked over to Joan, sat

down next to her and said, “Now listen to me, I really don’t care if these stories are true. All I care about is your well-being—your health. Albert and Mary care about your health too. They wouldn’t have come to me if they didn’t think I could help you.”

Joan started rocking back and forth on the couch and said, “They wanted you to help me, but I’m not sick. I’m healthy. That alien abduction story is not true. And, the story about me making loud noises when I pray to God is false. I’ve never prayed that loud. Why would Albert and Mary say such things?”

Dr. Wilborn placed his hands on her shoulders to stop her from rocking back and forth, and said, “You know good and well that Albert and Mary want nothing more than to help you. They love you too much to fabricate such tales. I did explain to Albert and Mary that the Zoloft I prescribed to you might have caused these problems. That medicine might have caused you to hallucinate ... maybe even caused you to forget. You know ... loss of memory. Maybe I should take you off of it. You have been taking that Zoloft for almost four-years now.”

“I don’t think I’ve been hallucinating ... nor had any memory lapses. Everything seems fine. Besides, your medicine has really been helping me. I don’t feel depressed anymore. I would have completely fallen apart after my parents died if not for that medicine.”

“I know you feel okay, and you think that

everything is fine, but your mind could be playing tricks on you," Dr. Wilborn replied. "You really could be having hallucinations, or experiencing memory loss. The Zoloft may be the cause of this. Just to play it safe, I want you to discontinue taking that medicine. I think you've been taking it long enough and it's time to stop. The Zoloft did help eliminate your depressive state, but it's probably causing you to have other problems ... such as hallucinations and memory loss. Joan, please don't blame all of this on Albert and Mary. They only want to help you. If you want to blame anyone for this, blame me. I shouldn't have kept you on the Zoloft for so long. Albert and Mary saw what you were going through and contacted me for assistance in the matter. I should have given you a milder drug to take or taken you off of that medicine sooner. That was my error in judgment."

"Don't blame yourself," Joan said. "You have always been there for me. You haven't done anything wrong. You're probably right about the Zoloft. Maybe that medicine is causing me to do and say strange things ... even hallucinate and forget. I refuse to believe that Albert and Mary would make up those stories about me. They love me and have been caring for me ever since my parents died. They have treated me as if I were their own daughter for years now."

Dr. Wilborn stood up, smiled and said, "Good, then everything is settled. Stop taking the Zoloft, and please keep in contact with me on a weekly basis. If you start feeling depressed, please call me or come right over to my office, and I'll prescribe a different type of medicine that will help you. We'll know if the Zoloft was the root cause of your problems after a couple of weeks. Also, Albert and Mary will let me know if you're still experiencing the same complications. I believe that after discontinuing the Zoloft, your problems will go away. So I really need your help, and Albert and Mary's help, concerning this matter."

Joan stood up, hugged Dr. Wilborn and said, "I will keep a daily diary of my activities and I will let you know on a weekly basis how I'm doing. I'll even ask Albert and Mary to notify you about any strange actions that I may exhibit during the next couple of weeks. I really do appreciate everything you do for me. Who knows ... if it weren't for Albert and Mary contacting you, my behavior may have gotten worse. I could have injured myself."

"That's right. I'm just glad that you understand why Albert and Mary contacted me. They meant no harm."

"I understand and appreciate everything that you're doing and Albert and Mary are doing for me. Thank you so much doctor."

"You're welcome, Joan," Dr. Wilborn said just before Joan left his office.

Dr. Wilborn still didn't know how to handle the accusation that Joan might have murdered her parents. It was hard to believe that Joan could do such a thing. His examination proved that they weren't murdered. And, Deputy Goony didn't see any signs of any foul play. Dr. Wilborn steadfastly believed that Albert and Mary were dead wrong in their belief that Joan murdered her parents.

8

Two weeks later, Joan was feeling much better after she stopped taking the Zoloft. Albert and Mary instantly noticed that Joan had discontinued her loud conversations with God, and her alien escapades were no more. Dr. Wilborn did not provide her with any more medications, and her trust and love for Albert and Mary grew even stronger. But deep in their hearts Albert and Mary still believed that Joan had murdered her parents. They just couldn't prove it.

9

The big day finally arrived, and Joan graduated from college with honors. On her graduation day, June 6, 2004, she felt as if she had outgrown Fall City and wanted to move on to a bigger city. That bigger city was Baltimore. Joan had always wanted to move to Baltimore to pursue her love for acting. She didn't know if her dreams of becoming an actor would come true, but she wanted to give it a try. Albert and Mary had happily agreed to move to Baltimore with her. Joan was only twenty-two-years-old and Albert and Mary wanted to keep the family together. Albert and Mary immediately put their home up for sale and prepared to leave with Joan. One month later, they found a buyer for their home and it was sold.

Dr. Wilborn, Sheriff McClotin, and Deputy Goony were shocked to find out that Joan, Albert, and Mary were all planning to move to Baltimore. They were saddened to see Joan move on, but they knew she would be happier pursuing her dreams. The night before Joan left for Baltimore she had dinner with Dr. Wilborn, Sheriff McClotin, and Deputy Goony at one of their three local restaurants.

Dr. Wilborn paid for Joan's meal, provided her with advice, and made her promise to call him, the sheriff, or the deputy if she had any problems in Baltimore. She promised to do just that. After finishing her meal, she said farewell to everyone while giving each one a hug.

10

It was six in the morning and still dark when Edith watched from behind a tree in the woods as Joan prepared to leave for Baltimore. Edith had just arrived when Joan had finished loading items onto the backseat of her car. Edith thought about hopping back onto her bicycle and quickly pedaling the fifty some yards to say good-bye to Joan, but she changed her mind because Joan looked as if she was in a rush. Edith was upset with herself because she had arrived too late to say her farewell. Edith watched as Joan got behind the wheel of her car and drove off. Even though Edith's eyesight wasn't as good as it used to be, it looked to her as if Albert and Mary weren't anywhere to be found.

As Edith watched Joan drive down the dirt road, something strange happened.

Joan had just driven a quarter of a mile down the road when her car suddenly stopped alongside the lake. Edith wondered if Joan had forgotten something and was planning to turn the car around, but the vehicle just sat there. Edith couldn't make out what was going on, so she started riding her bike toward the car.

11

Four Years Later (2008)

It was a cold, windy November morning in Baltimore when Joan decided to make a quick stop at the bridal and formal wear store before heading to work. She looked into the storefront window of the store in downtown Baltimore, smiled, and leaped for joy. The white bridal train dress was perfect, and the elongated back portion of the gown was the right length. She couldn't take her eyes off of the dress. This dress would categorically give Joan a majestic appearance on the day of her wedding. The price was a little more than she could afford, but the cost wouldn't matter once she found the right person to marry. She had worried that at twenty-six-years of age (almost twenty-seven) it would be too late to get married. But she'd stopped worrying after reading an article online that stated getting married at twenty-six was ideal. Furthermore ... this article emphasized getting a college degree before marrying, because educated individuals who marry are more stable than uneducated individuals who marry. Joan had found her dress, and all she needed now was a mate.

When Joan first arrived in Baltimore in August 2004, she immediately applied for a position as a law enforcement officer with the Baltimore Police Department. She did well on the physical exam and written test but excused herself after discovering how rigorous and time consuming the twenty-seven-week police academy was. Her hopes of becoming a cop had been vanquished, but she still needed to find work. So she applied for a bank teller position at a Wachovia bank and was hired. While working there, she never gave up on her love for acting. A few months later, she enrolled at The Buchanan Acting School (TBAS). The first four months of classes at TBAS were fantastic. Joan interacted well with the other students and got along fine with all the instructors. But things started to change for the worse.

After just four months of course work in self-exploration and improvisation, Joan became bored with the classes and dropped out of TBAS. All of a sudden, Joan lost interest in acting too, just as she'd lost her ambition to complete the police academy. Although Joan lost her passion for acting, she somehow found tranquility in working as a bank teller. Being a bank teller didn't pay very much, but she loved doing that kind of work, even though it was monotonous at times. Being a teller was a demanding job because it involved having a strong aptitude for numbers and handling large amounts of money. Joan had all the essential criteria to be a bank teller. She was discreet, trustworthy, punctual, and most importantly ... friendly. Talking to people and helping them was one of Joan's favorite things to do. She was very thorough in her work and avoided making any errors. She enjoyed meeting and greeting customers, as well as helping them with their monetary transactions. She just enjoyed being a plain old bank teller.

It was seven-thirty in the morning when Joan pulled into the Wachovia Bank parking lot, parked her car, and walked toward the bank's main entrance. Joan had been working as a bank teller at the Wachovia Bank in Baltimore, Maryland, ever since she moved from Fall City with Albert and Mary back in August 2004. It was now November 2008.

After entering the bank, Joan hurried over to her station and sat down adjacent to Cindy Hollaway.

"Good morning, Cindy," Joan said.

"Good morning, Joan. We have about fifty-five-minutes before the customers start to pile in. I'm so glad today is Friday."

"I'm glad too. Hey ... are you and Robert still planning to come over to my place this evening?"

"We sure are," Cindy said. "Is six p.m. okay with you?"

"That'll be fine," Joan replied.

At seven-fifty-five Joan and Cindy started counting their working cash for their drawers.

Their count of the money had to be accurate every time. As bank tellers, they were responsible for always handling their money in a safe and secure manner.

Ten-minutes later, their head teller, Kim, came over to verify their cash amounts.

"Good morning, ladies," Kim said.

"Good morning, Kim," Cindy and Joan replied simultaneously.

"I'll verify Cindy's cash amount first, and then yours, Joan."

Kim quickly but efficiently verified both Cindy's and Joan's working cash amounts to be accurate.

"Okay ladies, if you run into any problems, difficulties, or need to access the vault, just call me," Kim said before leaving.

It was eight-thirty when the rush of people started piling into the bank. Joan and Cindy wasted no time in assisting their customers. During their eight-hour workday, Joan and Cindy provided information about bank products and services; answered questions, helped customers solve their problems, set up new accounts, and provided all sorts of monetary transactions. The day ended up very much like every Friday did—with hundreds of checks being cashed and numerous deposits and withdrawals being made. Joan and Cindy, at the end of their workday, meticulously counted the cash they had on hand, listed the currency-received tickets on their balance sheet, made sure that all accounts were balanced, sorted all checks and deposit slips, and organized all paper records from their workday. After completing their work, they looked at one another and laughed. They both were glad it was time to go home.

12

As Jim Benson sat at one of the break room tables, eating his lunch, he thought about his future with the United States Postal Service as a limited-duty letter carrier. In twelve months he could retire with twelve years of service at age fifty-six. Jim knew his retirement pension wouldn't amount to much, but it didn't matter, because the pain in his lower back and feet were getting worse by the day.

Besides the issues with his lower back and feet, Jim had other problems. He had to deal with a manager who didn't know what he was doing or how to deal with carriers and clerks. The chaos at Marva View Post Office wasn't always the manager's fault, but this manager ascribed for about 90 percent of the problems. The other 10 percent of confusion could have been accredited to the carriers, clerks, and postmaster. No one was perfect when it came to doing his or her job at Marva View. There were times when carriers argued with carriers, clerks argued with other clerks, and carriers argued with the clerks. But most of the arguments were directed at management from both the carriers and the clerks. Marva View was a hot mess, along with hundreds of other post offices throughout the country.

Jim Benson stood six feet tall and weighed 210 pounds. His doctor had specifically pointed out that gaining weight wasn't an option after back surgery and foot surgery. If he gained any extra weight, his doctor explained, it could cause more pain in Jim's lower back and feet.

Jim ate his salad, drank his green tea, and thought about the Mega Million Lottery. Earlier today he'd purchased ten tickets in anticipation of winning the $105 million jackpot tonight. If he won, his problems would be over—at least with the postal service. Jim knew his chances of winning were slim to none, but he kept on playing, just like almost everyone else at Marva View. They all wanted to wake up the next morning after winning the lottery and never come back to the station again.

Billy walked in and sat down at the vacant table adjacent to Jim. Billy was also a limited duty letter carrier who worked with Jim. He was a hothead, a troublemaker, and a bully. Billy was five feet ten and weighed a hefty 230 pounds. His large round head, huge rubbery face, and humongous potbelly, was a testament to his out-of-control eating habits. Besides being obnoxious and gluttonous, Billy seemed to always find something to complain about.

"The only one who is doing work around here is me. You and Nelly need to step it up," Billy said to Jim before grabbing a handful of potato chips from his family-size bag of Lay's and taking a bite out of one of the four hot dogs he had brought for lunch.

Jim stopped eating, turned toward Billy, and said, "Just because you work a bit faster doesn't mean that Nelly and I aren't working just as hard as you are. Working fast doesn't always make things right. Remember: you made a critical mistake when you rushed putting those case labels up last week. In your rush to finish up and go home, you left out one row of addresses. You need to slow down and focus on what you do around here and quit making snide remarks about what everybody else is doing—particularly me and Nelly."

"So what ... I made a mistake. You know good and well that you and Nelly aren't perfect," Billy responded before eating his handful of potato chips and sipping his two-liter plastic container of Pepsi Cola.

"I can't speak for Nelly, but I know I'm not perfect. I make my fair share of mistakes like everybody else, but I'm getting tired of you running around and telling everyone that you're doing all the work in the office and Nelly and I are screwing off," Jim said.

"I'm tired of doing the majority of the work around here while you and Nelly do just enough to get by," Billy responded.

"Just worry about what you do for now on. Your constant nagging about what everybody else is doing is getting on my nerves. Again, some of us don't work as fast as you do, but we don't make as many mistakes as you do either," Jim replied.

Jim went back to eating his lunch while Billy scowled and took three quick gulps of his soda. Billy burped and then commenced to chow down on his second hot dog as if their conversation had never happened.

As Jim ate his lunch, he reminded himself about Billy's temper. He had to be careful how he spoke to Billy because of what happened between Billy and a clerk named Randy two weeks earlier in this very break room: *Randy had come into the break room and searched through the refrigerator for his soda, but he couldn't find it. Randy had a ham sandwich, and he badly wanted to chase it down with his soda. After a few more seconds of searching through the refrigerator he noticed an un-opened two-liter bottle of Pepsi Cola that belonged to Billy. Randy didn't realize that it belonged to Billy ... so he opened it. Randy was on his second cup of Pepsi Cola when Billy walked in. Billy immediately opened the refrigerator and noticed that his soda was gone. It was easy to notice that it was missing because Billy was the only person at the station to bring in a two-liter bottle of Pepsi Cola every day. Billy slammed the refrigerator door shut, turned in the direction of Randy and noticed his two-liter bottle of Pepsi cuddled up next to Randy. Billy stormed toward him, grabbed his bottle of soda with one hand, and grabbed the back of Randy's shirt collar and lifted him up and out of his chair. Randy dropped his cup of soda and ham sandwich and commenced to scream. After Billy lectured him about taking his soda, while he was holding him up by the collar, Artie, their supervisor, came in and made Billy put Randy down. Randy apologized to Billy and promised never to drink his soda again. Billy accepted his apology, sat down, and acted as if nothing ever had happened as he ate his lunch.*

Jim laughed, to himself, after remembering what happened to poor Randy that day. Jim finished his lunch and was cleaning his area up when he noticed Billy stuffing the remains of his fourth hot dog into his mouth and then scooping out the remaining pieces of potato chips from the bottom of the bag. Billy quickly chased that last hot dog and mouthful of potato chips down with a long gulp from his Pepsi Cola. After Billy tossed his hot dog wrappers, empty bag of potato chips, and empty bottle of Pepsi into the wastebasket, he purchased three Snicker bars from the vending machine and ate all three in less than a minute. Jim shook his head in disbelief and walked back to his work area after finishing up in the break room.

As Jim sat at his case, he started thinking about the injuries that prevented him from delivering his entire route. If he didn't have all those work-related injuries, he would have been able to deliver his entire route without any assistance. He wished that he were just a mailman that was free of injuries and pain once again.

Six-years ago Jim had experienced a work-related back injury that prevented him from delivering any mail until after he had back surgery. Even after having back surgery, he could only deliver a portion of his route. Even though that portion of his route was a light workload ... he still had lower back pain. Unfortunately for Jim, that back injury was the start of his limited-duty status.

Carrying a reduced portion of his mail route went well for Jim for a while, but then his feet started to hurt along with his back. This caused him to develop bunions on both of his feet, as well as metatarsal problems. He ultimately had surgery on his left foot, and this also hampered his delivery of the mail.

He was later subjected to working in the office and placing mail in the cases of various routes, answering the phone, running mail out to other letter carriers, and assisting the supervisor and manager with numerous tasks. Ultimately he was able to do collections, deliver express mail, and deliver mail to apartment complexes, businesses, and some residential areas.

Jim was often working inside the post office for most of the day because of his limited-duty status, and he hated that. Although he hated working indoors, there were other things that got under his skin. One of the hardest things for Jim to swallow was how uninjured carriers treated him. It was hard at first because many of the carriers thought he was faking his injuries, but he ignored the comments and innuendos that seemed to come up every day. One of the few people who understood what he was going through, besides the other limited-duty people, was Artie, his supervisor. Artie was sympathetic to Jim and other limited-duty personnel and did his best to work them within their limitations. Artie was probably one of the hardest working and most intellectual supervisors in Baltimore. He clearly understood Jim's disability issues.

On some days, Jim had to take Vicodin and Motrin just to ease the pain in his lower back and feet after standing for an hour or more. Just walking from his car in the parking lot to his work station in the post office induced discomfort. Casing mail on a daily basis also aggravated his lower back and feet. The constant bending and twisting irritated his back and feet even more, but he kept working. Jim and the other limited-duty carriers sometimes endured the pain by ignoring it because they wanted to get the job done without being labeled a whiner or crybaby. All the limited-duty letter carriers did their jobs to the best of their abilities.

13

The traffic was heavy on Friday afternoon, and it took Joan almost one hour to drive home from work rather than the usual thirty-minutes. After arriving at her condominium, she fed her puffer fish, took a shower, and put on a pair of jeans, and a sweatshirt. She went into her kitchen, where she removed a platter of thinly sliced Boar's Head salami, turkey, chicken, and cheese from her refrigerator. She carried the platter into her living room along with a box of Wheat Thins and placed the platter down on the living room table and carefully emptied the box of Wheat Thins onto the platter.

"Its five-forty-five," Joan said as she sat down near her fish tank to admire her puffer fish. Ten-minutes later, she picked up her phone and was about to call Cindy when her doorbell rang. She placed the phone back in its cradle, went to her front door, looked through the peephole, and opened the door. The cold air rushed in, causing her to shiver.

"Hey Baby ... am I the last to arrive?" Jim asked before kissing her on her lips.

Joan smiled, closed the door, and said, "You're the first to arrive. It sure feels colder than thirty two degrees. Hey, how come you didn't use your key to open the door?"

"I forgot and left them at my place. I'm glad you opened the door as quickly as you did. I was freezing. With the wind chill it's a bone-chilling twenty five degrees. I should just move in with you and I wouldn't have to worry about traveling in weather like this anymore," Jim said.

Joan lightly punched him on his shoulder, crossed her arms across her chest, and said, "So, why haven't you moved in?"

Jim paused for a moment, rubbed his chin, and said, "I just don't want to impede on your privacy. Besides, I still like going to my place, kicking off my shoes, and stretching out on my couch without being bothered after a hard day's work."

Joan smiled and said, "Oh, in other words, you don't want to be disturbed by some crazy woman when you come home from work every day."

"Exactly, but if I'm going to be nagged at by some crazy woman, I would rather it be you. All jokes aside, one day I will be asking you to let me move in with you," Jim replied.

"I'm looking forward to that. Just let me know when. Hey, how about grabbing me a beer out of the fridge?" Joan said.

"Okay."

"I can't believe Thanksgiving is just one week away. The weatherman said there will be colder temperatures and snow on Thanksgiving Day."

"I sure hope not," Jim said after removing his jacket and hanging it up in the hallway closet.

Jim walked into the kitchen, retrieved two bottles of beer, opened them, and carried them into the living room, where Joan had already taken a seat on the couch. Jim handed Joan her beer before sitting down next to her.

Joan placed her arm over his shoulders and said, "I missed you today. What took you so long to get here?"

Jim sighed and said, "Well, after I got off from work, my back started to really hurt, so I decided to take a hot bath when I got home. I didn't want to take any pain medication, because I knew I had to drive over here. Plus I had planned on drinking a few beers while I was here. Alcohol and drugs just don't mix."

Joan kissed him on his cheek and said, "You are so right. Consuming alcohol and drugs at the same time would be a deadly combination. Did your hot bath alleviate any of your back pain?"

"The bath did help, but being with you makes me feel much better," Jim said as he grabbed some Wheat Thins and a couple pieces of salami from the platter.

"Why thank you. I have those leftover chicken wings in the fridge if you want something else to eat," Joan responded with a huge smile across her face.

"No. This will be okay for now. Hey, when am I going to meet Albert and Mary? They have been promising to visit us, but they've always canceled their visits at the last minute," Jim said.

"They never really liked Baltimore. The first couple of months after we arrived here from Fall City, they decided to leave. They kept complaining about how big the city was. They couldn't take all the automobile traffic, the tall buildings, or the hundreds of people who crowded the streets every day. Two months later, on that heartbreaking Saturday morning, I woke up and found them packing up their luggage to move back to Fall City, and they did just that. I tried to talk them out of it, but it was useless. I drove them to the Greyhound Bus station and they left. It was one of the hardest things that I ever had to do. It was like losing my parents all over again. I cried like a baby when they boarded that bus and left."

"It's a shame I didn't get to meet them before they moved out of your condominium. Do you think they will ever visit us?"

"I forgot to mention this," Joan said, "but I talked to them by phone yesterday. They'll probably come up for Christmas, but they're not one-hundred-percent sure right now, because they still have a fear of big cities. I hope they come, because I really do miss them. They took me in and allowed me to live with them after my parents died. They really took good care of me."

"If they don't come up for Christmas, maybe we could take a vacation and go visit them," Jim said.

"That would be great! I'll give them a call later tonight to let them know we'll be planning to visit them in the future."

"I think they would enjoy our visit," Jim said.

"They would love it," Joan replied just as her doorbell rang. "That has to be Cindy and Robert." She leaped up from the couch and dashed to her front door where she quickly opened it, but stood behind it to avoid the incoming cold air.

"Hey guys," Joan said as she let them in.

"Hey ... Cindy and Robert," Jim said.

Both Cindy and Robert greeted Joan and Jim after coming in. Joan immediately closed the door behind them, took their coats, and started to hang them up in her hallway closet. As Joan hung up the coats, she thought back to the time when she and Cindy took their lunch break together after meeting at the bank for the first time. After Joan explained her experience growing up in Fall City, Cindy gave her a quick background about herself and Robert:

Cindy and Robert had been born and raised right there in Baltimore. They met while attending Morgan State University and fell in love during their sophomore year. Before their junior year of college started they dropped out and got married. Robert took a job as a car salesman at a Volkswagen dealership, and Cindy went to work at Wachovia Bank. They had been married for seven- years.

Robert and Cindy took a seat next to one another on the couch at the same time Joan sat back down next to Jim.

"I want to thank you and Cindy, once again, for introducing me to Joan four-years ago back on October 3, 2004," Jim said.

"Cindy and I thought that Joan would be a good match for you, so we decided to invite you and Joan over for dinner that day," Robert replied. "The rest is history."

"I'm so glad I met you," Jim said after giving Joan a hug.

"I love you so much," Joan replied before giving him a kiss.

Jim smiled, looked over at Robert, and said, "Hey, how many cars did you sell this past week?"

Robert hastily grabbed some Wheat Thins, some turkey, some cheese, and said, "Excuse me, Jim, but I need to get something to drink to go along with this food before I start talking about my place of employment. Boy, a cold beer would be great right about now."

Cindy laughed, turned to Robert, and said, "I'll go get us a couple of beers."

Cindy and Joan stood up and made their way into the kitchen. Joan sat down at the kitchen table while Cindy removed two beers from the refrigerator.

"I know you don't want to hear those two talk about car sales and sports," Cindy said.

"I sure don't," Joan answered.

"I'll be right back after I give Robert his beer," Cindy said after placing her own beer down on the kitchen table and walking back into the living room to hand Robert his.

"Thanks, honey."

"You're welcome," Cindy said before heading back into the kitchen.

After twisting off the top and taking a long swig from the bottle, Robert said, "Now, to answer your question about how many cars I sold this past week. I only sold one lousy car. That adds up to three sold for this entire month, giving me a total of fifteen hundred dollars. With Cindy's income we'll be okay monetarily even if I don't sell another car this month."

"Man, it must be a pain in the rear end trying to sell people cars with the way our economy is now. I can't imagine what you must go through to sell those Volkswagens. You must really love what you're doing," Jim said.

"I really enjoy my work, but selling cars is not an easy job. A typical day for me at work starts off with checking the cars for any vandalism that might have happened overnight. If nothing is wrong with the cars, I then ensure that they are clean and looking good for that day. For the remaining part of my day, I'm usually on the phone, talking to people who have either come by before, looking to buy a car, or have recently purchased a car from me. I normally ask them—the customers who've purchased a car from me—if they have any more questions about their newly purchased vehicle or if they are having any problems with their car. I often contact the customers, who haven't purchased a car, to come back by and take another look ... you know ... to purchase a car. I also implore them to tell their friends and family members about the great, reliable, low-priced cars at our Volkswagen dealership."

"And you've been doing this for how many years now?" Jim asked.

"Ever since Cindy and I've been married. I'm planning to ultimately become the new car sales manager."

"I don't have any doubt that you'll eventually make new car sales manager," Jim said. "If you can sell cars in this economy, you can do anything. You could even become a carrier supervisor or manager at a local post office."

Robert cringed, took another drink of his beer, and said, "No thanks. The horror stories I hear from you about the post office are enough to keep me away. I couldn't stomach working as a supervisor or manager in that organization ... nor could I carry any mail."

They both laughed, and then Jim turned on the TV and searched for something interesting to watch.

Cindy sat down at the kitchen table, opened her beer, and thought back to the time that she and Robert started hanging out with Joan and Jim.

The first time they all went out together, they went to see Paul Mooney at the Funny Bone comedy club, and they loved the show. The food and drinks were great, and Paul Mooney was hilarious. That night, Robert and Cindy really bonded with Jim and Joan. After that outing at the Funny Bone, they started to hang out on a regular basis. On most weekends, Cindy and Joan were always around one another. They were seen together at beauty salons, grocery stores, aerobics classes, and various restaurants. They were inseparable at times. The same could be said for Robert and Jim. A lasting friendship had developed between the two couples.

"Cindy, are you going to drink that beer or just hold it?" Joan asked.

Cindy stopped reminiscing about the great times she and Robert had had with Joan and Jim, took a sip of her beer, and said, "Sorry ... I was just daydreaming a bit. Hey, will you be able to attend that Tupperware party on Monday night?"

"Sure will. Jim and I don't have any plans for Monday."

"Great. I'll be over to pick you up at seven-thirty," Cindy said.

"I'll be ready."

Realizing, two beers later, that Wheat Thins, lunch meat, and a couple pieces of leftover chicken wasn't going to be enough to get them through the night, Cindy and Joan fixed a large pot of spaghetti and meatballs. They warmed up some garlic bread, prepared four plates, called the men into the kitchen, and started to eat.

They were having so much fun together that they all lost track of the time. It was a little after midnight when Cindy and Robert decided to go home. Joan tried to talk them into spending the night, but Robert promised they would spend the night some other time. Cindy wanted to stay, but Robert had to go to work at the Volkswagen dealership in the morning.

Cindy and Robert thanked Joan and Jim for the wonderful evening they had, said their goodnights, and left for home.

14

That Saturday morning, while at work, Robert dialed his home phone number, and after the third ring the voice mail picked up. It was the voice of Cindy saying: "*We're not home now; please leave your name and phone number, and we'll call you back as soon as possible.*" This was the third time Robert had called home and the third time the voice mail had picked up. Robert left a voice message for Cindy on all three occasions. He even tried calling Cindy's cell phone, but it automatically went to voice mail also.

"Where is that woman? It's ten in the morning, and she isn't picking up on either phone," Robert said as stress lines formed on his forehead while he sat at his desk.

So far he and Marion, the other car salesman, were facing a slow Saturday morning at their Volkswagen lot. While Robert and Marion waited for customers to show up, their manager, Anthony, was busy working in his office, inputting data into his computer. Marion realized how slow business was, so he started calling previous customers who had obtained Volkswagens, to see if any of their friends or relatives might be interested in purchasing one too.

Meanwhile, Robert was still concerned about Cindy: *She can't hear our home phone ringing because she's probably outside talking to one of our neighbors. And she might have forgotten to turn on her cell phone this morning after charging it the night before.*

Robert quit worrying about her after coming to the realization that Cindy was probably okay. He stood up and walked out onto the showroom floor and into the car lot after noticing two customers drive up. Robert knew he couldn't waste a second getting to a new customer, because Marion usually got to them first. He never could outrun Marion when it came to greeting customers, even though both of their offices were right next to one another. Marion had always darted out of his office as if it was on fire or someone was calling him late for dinner. Marion was constantly first on the scene when it came to the car buying customers.

As Robert stood in the car lot, he quickly looked back into Marion's office. Marion was reading from a folder on his desk and holding a phone to his ear. It looked as if Marion was talking a mile a minute as he shuffled some paperwork around on his desk. Robert was lucky today ... it was his turn to make a car sale.

Robert walked up to the customers after they exited their car and said, "Good morning ... I'm Robert Hollaway—new car salesman."

They both looked at Robert and paused.

Robert saw the scowls on their faces and their body language indicated that they didn't want to be bothered. Aspiring to be the perfect car salesman that he professed to be, Robert thought he could make them feel at ease with him. He extended his hand, and the male customer shook it.

"Hi, I'm David, and this is my wife, Minnie."

The word "wife" made Robert think about Cindy again, causing him to lose his train of thought.

Robert extended his hand towards Minnie, but she just walked away. David immediately made up an excuse to cover for Minnie's behavior by saying, "She's a little tired from the drive. We just got back in town, and we wanted to look at a few of your cars before we headed home."

"No need to explain. I totally understand ... what kind of car are you looking for?" Robert asked.

"None in particular. We really don't have any idea what we want to buy. We're just looking for now," David replied as he walked toward his wife.

Robert smiled, and his thoughts drifted back to Cindy again. He wondered where she could be at this hour.

Cindy always called Robert when he first started working for Volkswagen. She would call him two to three times a day during the weekdays, and numerous times when he worked on the weekends. Lately Cindy had dramatically cut back on her calls to Robert during the weekdays and on the weekends.

Robert followed behind David as if he were in a trance. He was in a befuddled state because he couldn't stop thinking about Cindy. At that moment, he completely lost interest in trying to sell this couple a car. He just wanted to call Cindy and hear her voice on the other end of the line.

Meanwhile ... David approached his wife and said, "Minnie, do you see anything you like?"

Minnie turned to answer him, but Robert was standing right next to David. Robert had his cell phone in his hand and was planning to call Cindy, but he changed his mind after Minnie gave him a menacing look.

Minnie frowned, grabbed David by his arm, and said, "I don't see anything I like." She pretended that Robert wasn't even there and pulled David toward another car. Robert continued to follow them even though it was evident that they wanted to be left alone.

Minnie found a car, checked the sticker price, and said, "David, this one costs twenty-four thousand, and it comes equipped with front, side-impact, and side-curtain airbags; three-point rear seat belts; power windows; power door locks; an AM/FM stereo, CD player, cruise control—"

"And power heated front seats," Robert said, interrupting her. "The best part about this car is that you'll get twenty-five miles to the gallon in the city and thirty-two miles to the gallon on the highway."

Minnie put both her hands on her hips, and turned toward Robert. David quickly stepped in between his wife and Robert before she could move any closer or say anything. David put his arm around her waist and led her toward their car. David's quick thinking and rapid reaction saved Robert from receiving a vicious tongue-lashing that he would have never forgotten.

"Robert, I think my wife and I will get on home now. We've been on the road for a while, and we need to go," David said.

Minnie's bottom lip was twitching with disgust, and the veins in her neck were standing out in livid ridges. She was visibly angry.

As Robert followed them to their car, he said, "I understand. But, when you decide to come back ... just ask for me."

Robert opened the front passenger-side door for David's wife, and she got in and sat down. Robert reached in to shake her hand and say good-bye, but Minnie closed the door so quickly that Robert almost had his fingers crushed in the door.

Robert's feelings were a little hurt, but he contributed Minnie's rudeness to the long drive that they had endured that day and their probable exhaustion. Robert followed David around to the driver side, where David opened the driver-side door, got in, sat down, and said, "Robert, have a good day."

David was about to shut his door when Robert reached into his pocket and handed David one of his business cards.

"Give me a call when you decide to purchase

one of our cars," Robert said after shaking David's hand.

David nodded, closed his door, started his car, and drove away. Robert looked at his watch and wondered why Cindy wasn't returning his calls.

15

Robert arrived home from work that Saturday evening at about seven o'clock and found his house empty. Cindy was nowhere to be found. Five-minutes after settling in, he saw a note taped to the refrigerator door saying that she was going to be at Kim's house for most of the day. Robert immediately used the phone in the kitchen and called Cindy's cell phone, but it went straight to her voice mail again. Robert quickly looked up Kim's phone number and called her. Robert asked Kim if Cindy was there, and she said yes, but she was using the bathroom. She told Robert that everything was okay and she would have Cindy call him back when she got out of the bathroom.

After hanging up, he felt much better knowing that Cindy was okay. He retrieved a bottle of water from the refrigerator, opened it up, and drank a quarter of it before heading into his living room. While waiting for Cindy to call he decided to open up the curtains to his living room window, but not before turning off the living room lights. He then moved his recliner next to his living room window and took a seat. He sat by his living room window, anxiously waiting for Cindy to call for twenty-minutes, but she didn't. Realizing that Cindy, for some reason, may have forgotten to call him he just sat there quietly in the dark. She maybe driving home right now, he thought, as he fidgeted nervously around in his recliner. With the lights being off, none of his neighbors could see him gaze out into the darkened and abandoned street via his living room window, biting his fingernails, while he waited for Cindy to arrive home. As he awaited her arrival, he became impatient after watching car after car drive by his home. There was no sign of Cindy. He bit his bottom lip and pounded his fists on the window ledge in desperation and anger. It was seven-thirty-five and neither his cell phone nor his home phone had rung since he'd called Kim. He didn't know what to do. Like a mannequin, Robert just sat in that chair next to his window and waited. By ten that evening, Robert had fallen asleep in his chair.

Robert was in a deep sleep ... he was dreaming that he and Cindy were at their church renewing their wedding vows. Just as Cindy was about to say *I Do* ... Robert was abruptly awakened by the sound of Cindy's car pulling into their driveway. It was one-fifty-five a.m. He leaped up from his chair, rushed over to the front door, and opened it. The headlights from the car temporarily blinded him before the car engine died. The next thing he heard was the car door being opened and then shut. The headlights shut off just as he heard the sounds of shoes impacting the concrete driveway.

The click-clacking of the shoes rang in his ears as it grew closer and closer to him. His vision cleared, and he smiled as Cindy quickly rushed by him and hurried straight for the kitchen. He closed the front door, followed her, and embraced and kissed her with all his might. He felt fantastic—as if the weight of the world had been lifted from his shoulders. He was happy again.

"You were at Kim's house all this time?" Robert asked as he took off her coat and placed it on one of the kitchen chairs.

"I hung out at her house all day," Cindy said as she prepared herself a gin and tonic.

"Cindy, that explains why you didn't answer the phone at home this morning, but I called your cell phone too."

"I accidentally left my cell phone off; that's why I didn't call you back. Hey, what's the big deal? I'm here now, and I'm okay."

"I'm glad that you're okay. I was worried about you. When I talked to Kim, she told me—"

"She told you that I was there, but I was using the bathroom at the time." Cindy said, interrupting him before gulping down her first gin and tonic. "She told you that everything was okay and that she was going to tell me to call you when I got out of the bathroom."

"But you didn't call me back," Robert said as he sat down at the kitchen table.

"Kim forgot to tell me that you called. She didn't tell me until I was already out the door at one-thirty this morning. I didn't even turn on my cell phone to call you, because I was on my way home. Plus I thought you would have been sound asleep by then."

Cindy poured herself another gin, this time without the tonic. She carried her glass into the living room and sat down on their couch. Robert followed her and sat down next to her, where he gently placed his arm over her shoulders and kissed her on her cheek.

"After you finish that drink, let's go to bed," Robert said as he pulled her close to him, causing her to spill most of her drink on the couch.

"Whoa! Look at what you did! Now I'll have to get another drink," she said as she quickly finished off what little gin she had left."

"I'm sorry, honey ... I didn't mean to do that. Go ahead and get another drink while I clean up this spill," Robert said before jumping up to retrieve some paper towels to clean up the spilled gin.

Cindy frowned and hastily went back into the kitchen and made herself another drink. Knowing that Robert wanted to get intimate ... she took a big sip of her gin and said, "Robert, why don't you go into the bedroom and I'll join you there in a few minutes."

Robert smiled, quickly cleaned up the spilled gin, and dashed into their bedroom, where he undressed and leaped onto the bed.

Cindy wanted to get blitzed because she knew she would have to make love to him tonight and the thought of it disgusted her. After her final glass of gin, she lackadaisically strolled into the bedroom, removed her clothes, and crawled into bed next to him.

As he made love to her, she fought back the disgust and hatred she held for him. Her stomach churned and ached while she swallowed back the vomit that tried to force its way out of her mouth. Once he finished, she pushed him aside, rushed into the bathroom, closed the door, and threw up into the toilet.

"Are you all right, Cindy?" Robert said as he leaned up against the bathroom door.

"Yes ... I am. I had a little too much to drink. I'm going to take a shower ... I'll be fine."

"Would you like some Pepto-Bismol, or Tylenol?"

"No thanks."

"Let me know if you need anything, honey ... I'm here for you," Robert said.

"I'll be okay," she said as she stepped into the shower, cowered in one corner, and began to quietly weep as the water ran through her hair and onto her body.

She wanted to leave Robert, but it wasn't going to be easy. Cindy just didn't know how to tell him, or when to tell him that she wanted a divorce. Telling Robert that she'd planned on divorcing him would break his heart, because he was madly in love with Cindy. Robert was overly protective of her because she was gorgeous. She was a full-figured woman of Amazonian stature who stood about six feet tall. Her lavishly endowed body, shoulder-length salt-and-pepper hair, clear caramel complexion, high cheekbones, sultry green eyes, and sensuous lips had every man after her. Poor Robert had no idea that she badly wanted to leave him.

16

Jim arrived home from work at five that afternoon, grabbed a beer from his fridge, and sat down at his kitchen table. After finishing his beer, he mixed a large amount of rum with some Coca-Cola in a glass and drank that too. Fifteen-minutes later, the alcohol didn't ease his pain, so he found his Percocet pills, took one, and chased it down with another beer. That did the trick; he immediately started to feel better. The agonizing pain that was in his lower back and both his feet were starting to dissipate. He felt minimal pain as he walked from his kitchen and into his living room.

He sat down on his couch, grabbed his remote, clicked on the TV, and searched the channels for something interesting to watch. He soon found a movie that involved a mailman who was murdering his customers. One of his victims was an elderly lady who invited him in so she could sign a certified letter. The woman made the fatal mistake of turning her back, on this mailman, while she was preparing to sign the letter. That's when this homicidal maniac went to work. He grabbed her by her frail shoulders, turned her around, and wrapped both of his hands around her neck. The elderly lady lost her balance, and they both fell to the floor. As he lay on top of her, he continued to strangle her until she stopped breathing. After she stopped breathing, he meticulously forced a screwdriver into her right ear.

Jim was mesmerized by this movie. This killer postman quickly left the house after murdering this little old lady and continued to deliver the mail as if nothing had ever happened. Although Jim was three sheets to the wind ... he moved to the edge of his couch to get a closer look at this crazed mailman in action. The title of the movie was: *The Killer Postman*. Jim watched the rest of the movie without moving a muscle. He couldn't believe that someone had actually made a movie about a murderous mailman. Jim reasoned, at the conclusion of the movie, that it wasn't too far-fetched that a postal worker would actually kill his or her customers. He knew postal employees had actually gone on murderous rampages in the past, but none had ever killed their customers.

Jim stood up, walked into his kitchen, and made himself another rum and Coke. After making his drink, he went to his bedroom, sat down on his bed, and thought about how screwed up his life was. Yes, he had a good job, good pay, and good benefits, but his mental and physical health was shot. Jim was fifty-five-years-old, but he felt as if he were in his late sixties. He guzzled down his drink, stretched out across his bed, and fell into a deep sleep.

Jim suddenly awoke and looked at his clock. It was nine-thirty in the evening. He instantly knew that he was in big trouble! He went into his bathroom, threw some cold water onto his face, and immediately dialed Joan's number.

"Hello," Joan said.

"Joan ... this is Jim. I'm so sorry that I overslept."

"I should have called you at seven to make sure you were here by seven-thirty for dinner tonight. I really was looking forward to seeing you."

"I screwed this whole evening up. I have to be truthful with you about this ... I forgot about our dinner date."

"No kidding!" Joan said. It was lonely and painful, but I ate dinner without you. Don't worry; I've wrapped up your plate and put it in the refrigerator. Maybe I'll see you tomorrow and you can eat it then. This is the third time you've stood me up this year. You know how much I enjoy our dinner date nights together."

Jim cleared his throat and said, "I'm so sorry, Joan. I came home from work, took a pain pill, had a few drinks, watched a movie, and fell asleep. I was so tired and in pain that I forgot about our date. I will make this one up to you by taking you out to dinner on a day of your choice."

"You'd better. Well, I'm too upset to continue this conversation, so I'm going to go to bed. I'll talk to you tomorrow. Good night." With that, Joan hung up the phone.

Jim felt so bad that he held the phone to his ear for a few seconds after Joan had hung up. He hadn't even gotten a chance to say good-night to her. He finally hung up the phone, took a shower, and went to bed.

17

Joan rested on her recliner, in the den, as she gazed out of her window and into her backyard. She was envisioning a lovely future with her lover, but worried about the fallout ... what everyone might say after finding out about her affair. She really didn't care because their plan was to get married, leave town, and start a new life. All she could think about was how much fun they had when they were together. She fought off the temptation to just sprint out of her condominium, leap into her car, and drive over to her lover's house. Instead of doing that ... Joan just decided to call.

She picked up the phone four times and quickly hung it back up each time without ever dialing a number. She clasped her hands together, gazed toward the ceiling, and rocked back and forth in her recliner. She grew skittish, and her entire body started trembling. Beads of sweat started to appear upon her forehead. To calm herself, Joan turned to the picture on the fireplace mantel piece and looked at the four of them together. Herself and Jim, Robert and Cindy were all sitting on the front porch settee at Cindy's parents' home. Robert was kissing Cindy on her forehead, and Joan and Jim were locked in a bear hug of affection. All four had decided to take a picture together as a memento of their everlasting friendship to one another. Instead of this picture soothing her, it struck terror in her heart. She feared that she would lose her dear friends once her scandalous love affair was discovered. That was the last thing she wanted to happen.

Joan remembered how deeply in love Cindy and Robert were years ago, but as time went on, things slowly started to change between Cindy and Robert, and they grew further and further apart. The same thing was happening with Joan and Jim eventhough Joan was trying desperately to make her and Jim's relationship work. She was in love with Jim and persisted on getting married, but Jim wanted to wait. Joan held out hope that Jim would change his mind and ask for her hand in marriage sooner rather than later, but year after year, Jim seemed to always avoid asking her to marry him. Joan started to seriously doubt that Jim would ever propose to her. Regardless of Jim's refusal to get married, he still deeply cared for and loved Joan just the same. Sadly, as the days, weeks, months, and years rolled on, Joan's feelings for Jim slowly dissipated. She gradually fell out of love with him. Joan tried desperately to keep her affection for Jim, but she started to lose her patience.

Joan hid her cheating ways so well that Jim never knew she had started to see someone else on a regular basis. Joan and her new lover had fallen madly in love and knew their secret love affair couldn't be revealed until they were ready. They never said a word about their undercover fling to anyone—not even to their best friends. At times, Joan struggled with her feelings for both her lover and Jim. It really troubled her to have love for the both of them. Joan felt like a snake; she just wanted to find a hole in the ground and crawl into it. Sadly, Joan wept over her situation many a night. She was caught in a love triangle that was sure to cause major problems. She knew it would break Jim's heart if he discovered she was having an affair, but it didn't matter, because her secret lover had promised that they would be married soon—and Joan was smitten.

Joan turned away from the picture and watched the squirrels scamper around in her backyard, but all she could think about was her new love interest.

"Hey Joan," Jim said as he suddenly appeared.

Startled and surprised by his sudden entrance, Joan turned toward Jim and said, "What are you doing here? You scared the heck out of me. I didn't even hear you come in. Plus I never expected you to come by today."

"I'm sorry baby. I didn't mean to scare you. I'm surprised you didn't hear me when I opened the front door. I called out your name before I entered, but you didn't answer. I came straight in here and found you sitting in your recliner. You looked like you were in a trance. It was as if you were asleep with your eyes open."

"I was thinking about Albert and Mary. I really miss them," Joan said after thinking of a lie to tell him.

"I know you miss them, but remember ... we're going to visit them soon. Everything will be fine. It'll be like a family reunion. I want you to be happy."

Joan sat still in the recliner, looked up at Jim, and said, "You really do care about me ... about how I feel."

"Of course I care. That's why I'm here now. I want to spend some quality time with you. The mail volume at work was light today, and I finished up early. That's when something came over me and I started thinking about you. Don't ask me to explain it, but all of a sudden I needed to be with you. After I finished delivering the mail on my route, I took an hour of annual leave and left work to be with you."

Joan jumped out of her recliner, wrapped her arms around Jim, and kissed him.

"What was that for?" Jim asked.

Joan smiled and said, "I'm so happy to hear that you wanted to spend some time with me. You really do love me."

"Of course I love you."

Joan grabbed Jim by his arm and guided him into her living room and over to her couch. "Sit down, young man, because I have to talk to you about something very important."

Jim sat down, and Joan sat down next to him. She grabbed Jim's hands and held them tightly with both of her hands. She took in a deep breath and looked Jim straight in his eyes. Jim was perplexed about the whole situation, but he remained patient.

There was silence for about twenty seconds, but to Jim it seemed like ten-minutes. Joan wanted to say her piece, but the butterflies in her stomach and her nerves had gotten the best of her. Jim noticed the urgency and fear in Joan's facial expression, and he broke the silence.

"What's going on? You're starting to scare me," Jim said.

Joan realized she had gone about this whole thing wrong because she had startled Jim. She saw the concerned look on Jim's face, heard the desperation in his voice, and said, "I didn't mean to scare you. I just wanted to know if you will ever marry me."

Jim removed his hands from Joan's grip, kissed her on her cheek, and said, "I love you with all my heart, but I'm not ready to get married."

Joan's shoulders slumped, her eyes widened, and a snarl of agony spread over her face. "Okay. So when do you want to get married? We can find a justice of the peace and get married anytime. We've been dating for a little over four years now. I'm not getting any younger, you know."

"I plan on retiring from the United States Postal Service in twelve months. I want to marry you after I retire. By waiting to get married, after I retire, I'll be able to figure out what my retirement pay will be. Baby, I just want to make sure that I'll be able to take care of you financially," Jim replied.

"I didn't know you wanted to retire from the postal service. Why didn't you tell me?"

"I didn't tell you because I wasn't quite sure if I was going to retire, but now I believe I will retire in twelve months."

"That's great news," Joan said.

"We would be fine financially—if we got married right now, but twelve months from now ... who knows. That's why I want to wait to see how things work out. Remember ... I'm only fifty-five-years-old, and I won't get a full Social Security check until I'm sixty-two-years of age. Who knows ... I may have to find another job to make ends meet after I retire. Joan, I'm begging you to hang in there for one more year."

Tears had started to roll down Joan's face. She crossed her arms across her chest, pouted, and said, "Jim, you want me to wait one more year? We can get married sooner than that. We'll make it. My job at the bank and your retirement pay will get us through. You can move out of your condo and into my condo, or I can move out of my condo and into yours. We can do it!"

Jim moved closer to Joan and placed his arm across her shoulders. He gave her a long, passionate kiss, wiped the tears off her cheeks, and said, "I know we could make it, but I want to wait another year before we get married to be certain."

Joan uncrossed her arms, and they clasped hands once again.

"You don't want to tie the knot right now," Joan nervously muttered.

Jim let out a sigh and said, "I don't, but you are the only woman I love. I just want you to promise me that you'll wait another twelve months before we get married."

Joan let go of Jim's hands and then she stood up. Her eyes took on a wounded look. She forced a smile onto her face and said, "I'll wait ... I'll wait for you."

Jim immediately shot up from the couch, wrapped his arms around her, pulled her close to him, and smiled. He was happy she'd promised to wait for him. But, Joan never wrapped her arms around him ... she just stood there motionless.

18

As Robert made love to Cindy, she continued to smoke her cigarette. She seemed oblivious to Robert's heavy panting, moaning, and constant sweating. After a minute into Robert's lovemaking, Cindy sighed and then flicked the ashes from her cigarette into the ashtray on the nightstand next to their bed. One minute later, Robert climaxed and Cindy finished her cigarette. Cindy pushed Robert off of her and rushed into the bathroom to take a shower. Robert was too spent to even notice that Cindy had despised the whole ordeal. He just rolled over onto his side and smiled, believing Cindy had enjoyed it too. During many of their future steamy encounters it didn't take Robert long to figure out that Cindy had lost all interest in him. She just stopped her physical and affectionate holding and cuddling of Robert during their love making. She simply let her arms fall to her sides and even avoided kissing him. Cindy would just lie there without even moving; it was as if she was a cold corpse spread out on a slab at a morgue. She even stopped kissing him good-bye in the morning when he left for work, and when he returned home from work. Their casual conversations quickly stopped during breakfast and dinner. If they did converse, Cindy made sure that it was short and to the point by responding with a two-to-three-word response. Robert was flummoxed.

Robert tried to salvage their marriage by seeing a marriage counselor, but Cindy wouldn't have any part of it. Going to those sessions would've been a waste of time for Cindy, because she had fallen totally out of love with Robert and wanted desperately to end their relationship as soon as possible. Robert refused to believe that his marriage was nearing its end, so he continued to lavish all his affection upon Cindy, but it was never reciprocated. Cindy loathed him and wanted absolutely nothing to do with him. Robert was a broken man.

19

"It's almost five p.m., and Joan will be upset with me if I don't feed her puffer fish," Jim said after getting up from the couch and making his way into Joan's kitchen.

He retrieved the fish food, went back into the living room, and fed the fish. After feeding the fish, he sat down on the living room couch, turned on the TV, and started watching the news. As he watched the news, he thought of a brilliant idea. He decided to give Joan a surprise birthday party. It was November 30, and Joan's twenty-seventh birthday was on December 15. Jim would have only fifteen days to plan for it, so he had to act fast. He thought about having it at his place, but Joan's condo was bigger, so he decided to have it there. But, there was one problem ... he had to keep Joan away from her condo most of that day. Someone had to keep her away for three to four hours starting about two o'clock that afternoon. And that someone was Cindy.

"Since Joan is out shopping and I'm babysitting her fish, I'll just make some calls," Jim said just before calling Cindy and Robert's home.

Robert took down the information about the surprise birthday party and passed that information onto Cindy. Jim also called other close friends of Joan's to let them know about the surprise birthday party he was planning for December 15. The surprise birthday party was all set after forty-five minutes of communicating on the phone with all of Joan's friends.

It would be Cindy's job to keep Joan away from her condo on the afternoon of December 15. The plan was to have Cindy trick Joan into leaving her condo around two o'clock and return at five-thirty that afternoon. By that time ... that would've given Jim and Robert enough time to set everything up and have all of Joan's friends and coworkers over when she returned home.

"This is going to be great. I'll have to call Reynold's Bakery to order her cake first, and then I'll start searching for a gift. I'll have Cindy and Robert help me get the food and party decorations a couple of days before Joan's birthday. And, I'll store all those items at my place until the day of the party. Robert and I, on the day of the party, will take all of the party items over to Joan's condo after Cindy tricks Joan into leaving," Jim said as he wrote down what he had to do to prepare for the surprise birthday party.

Jim thought of something else after writing down all the items he needed for the party. That something else would make Joan so proud of him. More importantly it would make the party so very special for Joan too.

"I'll invite Albert and Mary to Joan's birthday party. I know its short notice, but I'll even pay for their flight from Fall City, South Carolina, to Baltimore. We were planning on visiting them anyway, so why not have them fly here for Joan's birthday party."

Jim smiled at first, but his smile quickly turned into a frown. He had no way of contacting Albert and Mary, and he'd never personally talked to either of them. Jim only knew that they had moved back to Fall City. He could ask Joan for their phone number, but what excuse or lie could he possibly tell Joan to get their phone number? Joan called Albert and Mary once a month at a minimum, but she was very sensitive and private about her conversations with them. She never talked long, and she never let Jim speak to them, but she always was in the highest of spirits when chatting with them. She had the biggest smile on her face after every conversation with them. Jim always wanted to talk to Albert and Mary, but for whatever reason, Joan never let him.

As Jim pondered what to do about contacting Albert and Mary, he started to snoop around Joan's condo. He searched desk drawers in Joan's computer room; he searched her bedroom and searched her living room for any phone numbers with Albert's and Mary's names written beside them. After thoroughly searching her entire condo, Jim gave up. There weren't any phone numbers for Albert and Mary anywhere. He sat down on Joan's couch and sulked for a few minutes before he decided to call 411, directory assistance, to get the information number for Fall City, South Carolina.

After getting the information number for Fall City, he immediately dialed it. The phone rang two times before an elderly woman picked up the phone. It sounded as if she was in a tunnel as her voice echoed for the first ten seconds ... and then the echoing stopped. The operator's voice was lifeless and monotone.

"Fall City information operator. What number, please?"

"I would like to get the number for Albert and Mary Niphon. They live there in Fall City," Jim said.

"One moment, please. I'll look that number up. Sir, I'll have to put you on hold."

"Okay," Jim replied before the phone went silent.

A minute elapsed, and Jim thought he may have been disconnected. He rubbed his chin and wondered if the operator would ever return. Two-minutes later, the operator picked up the phone and said, "Sorry for the delay, sir, but we don't have an Albert and Mary Niphon listed. Maybe they just moved here and their number hasn't been added to our directory, or they might just have an unlisted number."

"I'm sure they live there. I believe they've been there for the last four years, but their number could be unlisted, as you mentioned," Jim said.

"That could be the case. We do have a few

citizens here with private numbers. I'll tell you what ... I'll connect you to our sheriff's office and let you talk to him. The sheriff knows everyone who lives here in Fall City."

"Thank you. I really appreciate that," Jim said.

"Good luck, sir," the operator said before connecting him to the sheriff's office.

The phone went silent for a moment and Jim thought he was cut off again, but he wasn't. Another voice responded on the other end within seconds.

"Sheriff McClotin's office ... Ruth speaking."

"Hello, is the sheriff available?" Jim asked.

"He won't be in for a couple of days. Who's calling?" Ruth asked.

"My name is Jim Benson, and I'm calling from Baltimore, Maryland. I'm trying to get in touch with an Albert and Mary Niphon. It's important that I talk to them."

"I would love to help you, but you could be a telemarketer, a bill collector, or a salesman trying to get information about some of our citizens. I'm not authorized to provide you with any information about our citizens without their approval," Ruth explained.

"Believe me; I'm not a salesman, telemarketer, or bill collector. Albert and Mary Niphon are good friends of my girlfriend; they are family to her. I just want to get a phone number in order to contact them."

Ruth paused and said, "I'll leave your phone number for Sheriff McClotin. He's under the weather right now, but he promised me that he would return to work in a couple of days. As soon as he comes in, I'll tell him to call you. You can explain your situation to him when he calls you. I'm terribly sorry, but I'm not allowed to give out any information concerning our citizens—especially their phone numbers or home addresses—unless authorized by them or, on rare occasions, the sheriff."

"I understand fully. Please don't forget to have him call me," Jim said after providing Ruth with his full name and home phone number.

"I certainly will. Sorry I couldn't help you."

"You have helped me by taking my number. I'll just wait for the sheriff to give me a call. Thanks so much."

Jim hung up, smiled and said to himself, "In a couple of days, I'll get the number from the sheriff for Albert and Mary. Once I get it, I'll immediately call them and invite them to the surprise birthday party for Joan. Joan will be so happy and thrilled to see them."

It was nine-thirty that evening when Joan arrived home.

"It's about time you got home," Jim said after giving her a hug and a kiss.

"Thanks for keeping my fish company."

"You're welcome," Jim replied.

"I didn't see anything I liked at any of the stores," Joan said.

"Wow. You mean to tell me you didn't spend any money?"

"That's right. Hey ... are you going to spend the night?" Joan asked.

"Not tonight. I have to be to work by six-thirty tomorrow morning. I want to get home, iron my uniform, and get to bed by ten-thirty."

"I was really counting on you to stay the night," Joan said.

"I would love to spend the night, but I have to arrive to work early tomorrow. I'll call you after I get off from work tomorrow. Remember: I'll be here by six p.m. tomorrow ... so be home," Jim said. He then kissed her on her forehead and dashed out the door.

20

It was five-twenty p.m. when Joan frantically arose from the bed, slid to the edge, and just sat there. She covered her face with both her hands and started to cry. Suddenly she heard the shower water stop, and she quickly wiped the tears from her face. She hastily dressed and was about to leave when the bathroom door swung open and her hand was grabbed. Joan tried to break free but stopped resisting and turned toward her lover. They looked into each other's eyes, hugged, and briefly kissed. Joan broke away from their embrace, opened the hotel room door, and dashed toward the elevator without even saying good-bye. As Joan waited by the elevator ... she thought about the zealous love she'd just made. The relationship she had with her newfound love made her feel dirty and ashamed. But the euphoria she experienced made it all worthwhile. She also thought of her relationship with Jim, which made her feel guilt-ridden.

It seemed like an eternity to Joan as she waited for the elevator door to open. As she waited, she turned and looked back toward the open hotel room door. To Joan's surprise, her lover stood there naked and motioning for her to come back in. At that instant, the elevator bell rang and the door opened. Joan quickly turned back toward the elevator, stepped in, pressed the lobby button, and watched the door close. The elevator's quick descent sent a rush through her body, and Joan thought about the great love she'd just made. She blushed and wished she were back in the hotel room again. The elevator bell rang once more, indicating that it had reached the lobby. The door opened, and two people got on before she ran out. She held her head down and tried to cover her face as she scurried through the crowded lobby, out the front door, and into the hotel parking lot, where she found her car. As she opened her car door, she prayed that none of her friends or Jim's friends had seen her. She started to panic even more when she thought of the possibility that Cindy's or Robert's friends may have seen her. She started to cry again, but she gained control of her emotions, wiped the tears away for the last time, and drove out of the parking lot towards home.

Thirty-minutes later, Joan unlocked her front door, entered, and rushed to see her fish. She stood right beside her fish tank and watched them swim wildly around before they noticed her. Once they noticed her ... they started to swim in her direction. As her fish marveled in her presence ... It seemed as if they were smiling at her. For that moment, Joan felt calm and joy as she gazed back at them. She smiled at them and touched the glass of the fish tank as if she were touching them. They all seemed happy to see her.

She wanted to bond with her fish all night, but she dragged herself away from her fish, went into the kitchen and removed two cans of beer from the refrigerator. She sat down at the kitchen table, popped open the first can, and took a drink. She removed her cell phone from her back pocket, turned it back on, and placed it on the kitchen table.

After finishing off the first can of beer, she opened the second. She guzzled down the second can just as quickly as the first, tossed the cans into the trash can, and pondered what to do next. She looked at her phone on the wall in her kitchen and decided to call Jim as soon as she got up enough nerve to tell him that it was over. She wanted to tell him that she'd found someone new and that they were going to get married, but was hesitant to do so.

She decided against calling him because it would be cowardly to give Jim the bad news over the phone. She knew that eventually she would have to tell him, but it wasn't going to be over the phone! If she was going to tell Jim ... it would have to be face-to-face. Besides, Jim was supposed to come by at six to visit her today and she considered telling him then. It was five-minutes after six and she worried Jim wasn't going to show up. At six-eleven she heard her front door open and then close. Jim walked directly into the kitchen, carrying a bag, and kissed her on her cheek.

"I hope you're not mad with me," Jim said. "It's eleven-minutes after six, and I told you I'd be here by six today."

Joan smiled and said, "Don't be silly; I'm just glad you're here."

"Hey, where have you been? I called your cell phone and your home phone earlier today, but your voice mail picked up. And, you never returned my calls."

Jim placed the large bag on the kitchen table, grabbed a beer from the refrigerator, sat down next to Joan, and put his arm over her shoulders.

Stress lines formed on Joan's forehead, her bottom lip started to twitch, and her facial expression was gaunt with worry, but she took in a deep breath and said, "I was ... I was at Bronson's Mall, shopping at Dillard's and Macy's. I tried to call you, but I couldn't pick up a signal with my cell phone. I just got here about ten-minutes or so before you walked in."

Jim reared back and raised one of his eyebrows in a questioning slant. He gave Joan a look of uneasy puzzlement and said, "You're a bit tipsy. Did you have something to drink today?"

"Two beers," Joan responded with a sheepish smile.

Jim moved closer to her and said, "Two beers is your limit. No more beers for you tonight, young lady."

Joan smiled and said, "I agree ... no more beers for me."

Jim returned the smile and said, "That's my

girl. Hey ... yesterday, when I was sitting here all alone, I thought about your upcoming birthday. I want to do something special for you. I want to take you out to dinner."

Joan's eyes widened incredulously, and she said, "That is so sweet of you. I would love to do that."

"Well then, that's settled. But now let's talk about tonight. First of all, I would never miss a Saturday night date with you. I show up here every Saturday evening at six, like clockwork. I figured I would call you first to see what you wanted for dinner, but I gave up when I couldn't get in touch with you. So I went ahead and purchased us some Chinese food," Jim said.

Joan leaned toward him, kissed him on his cheek, and said, "Thanks for bringing the food ... I'm famished."

"You're welcome. Somebody has to take care of you. You know I'm always thinking about you."

Joan was full of cheer as they removed the three boxes of food from the bag, opened them up, and started to eat. Ten-minutes into eating their dinner, Jim said, "Have you heard from Albert and Mary lately? Remember ... we're going to visit them soon."

Joan grabbed a steamed dumpling out of one of the boxes, took a bite of it, raised her hand to tell Jim to wait one minute, gulped the remaining dumpling down, and said, "Funny you should mention them. They called me today just before I left on my shopping spree. They really can't wait to meet you. Oh, I did tell them about our plans to visit them soon."

"That's great. I'm looking forward to seeing them too. I want to tell them that I'm so glad that they took such good care of you. And, if it wasn't for them ... I might have never met you," Jim replied.

Joan almost burst into tears, but she bit her bottom lip to prevent herself from crying right in front of Jim. She felt so ashamed for cheating on him. At that moment, she wanted to run into the bedroom and lock the door, but she put on a fake smile and continued as if she wasn't having an affair.

Jim suspected something was wrong—unusual—because of Joan's consumption of beer and her demeanor. She might have had a bad day and didn't want to talk about it. That would explain why she'd had the two beers. He attributed her unusual facial expressions and odd body language to the two beers and bad day she may have experienced. But, he ignored those thoughts because Joan seemed to cheer up. She smiled at him and continued to eat. As she ate, she decided not to tell Jim that it was all over just yet and wondered if she was making the right decision to leave Jim.

21

"Hello," Jim said after picking up his phone. There was silence for a second before the voice on the other end said, "This is Sheriff Mike McClotin calling from Fall City, South Carolina. Can I speak to Jim Benson?"

Jim was glad that the sheriff returned his call. He was starting to worry because he had only thirteen more days to go before Joan's surprise birthday party.

"I'm Jim Benson. Thanks for returning my call, Sheriff McClotin."

"You're welcome. This is my first day back to work after dealing with a bad cold, so I figured I would call you after I straightened out a few minor issues here in my fair city first. I feel a whole lot better now. I believe the cold I caught is just about out of my system."

"I'm glad to hear that you're feeling better. I don't want to hold you up, but is it possible to get a phone number for Albert and Mary Niphon? I know that I'm a total stranger to you, but I'm dating Joan Witherspoon. Joan used to live in Fall City before she moved here to Baltimore a little over four years ago. I know this sounds odd, but I want to contact Albert and Mary to invite them here, to Baltimore, for Joan's birthday party," Jim said.

"Albert and Mary Niphon!" Sheriff McClotin said.

"Yes ... Albert and Mary Niphon," Jim replied.

The sheriff cleared his throat and said, "You say you're dating Joan Witherspoon."

"Yes," Jim replied.

"Hasn't she told you that Albert and Mary moved to Baltimore with her?"

"Yes, she did, but she said they moved back to Fall City after a couple of months of living here in Baltimore. She personally drove them to the bus station the day they left Baltimore. Joan has been living by herself ever since they left," Jim said.

Sheriff McClotin said, "Something isn't right. Albert and Mary Niphon never moved back to Fall City. I haven't seen or heard from Joan, Albert, or Mary for a number of years now. The last time I saw or even spoke to either of them was before they all moved to Baltimore. Besides, Albert and Mary's home has been occupied since they left for Baltimore. The Nelson family lives there now."

"Sheriff, you must be mistaken, because Joan has called and talked to Albert and Mary many times since they moved back to Fall City," Jim said.

"Mr. Benson, I'm telling you that she wasn't calling Fall City, because Albert and Mary haven't lived here for years. They probably moved to some other city and you got it mixed up with Fall City."

"Sheriff, believe me, Joan specifically told me that they live in Fall City. We were even planning on coming to Fall City to visit them," Jim said.

The sheriff laughed for a moment and said, "Is this some kind of practical joke? Let me speak to Joan. We'll get this problem ironed out right away."

"She's not here. You see, Joan's birthday is on December 15, and I was trying to plan a surprise birthday party for her with Albert and Mary as surprise guests. I don't want Joan to know that I was trying to contact them."

"Well, young man, that would be quite some surprise—especially if you locate Albert and Mary Niphon here in Fall City. I'll tell you right now they are not in Fall City. If they aren't in Baltimore, I don't know where they are. I suggest you ask Joan for the phone number for Albert and Mary without letting on about your surprise birthday plans. In the meantime, please tell Joan I said hello and have her give me a call when she gets a chance. I would love to talk to her, and so would some of the other Fall City residents who haven't heard from her since she moved away."

"Sheriff, I would love to tell her to call you, but I don't want her to know I've called Fall City or even talked to you about Albert and Mary Niphon. I'll have to find a way to get the phone number from Joan without her catching on. Sheriff, I promise

I will have her call you the day after her surprise birthday party."

"Thanks. I sure hope you get this whole thing straightened out. I'll be listening for Joan's call after her birthday party. Take care, young man." The sheriff hung up the phone.

Jim hung up his phone and sat down. He was baffled. He could have sworn that Joan had told him that Albert and Mary moved back to Fall City. He had only thirteen days to contact Albert and Mary before Joan's birthday, and time was running out.

22

Sheriff McClotin arrived at work the following morning, sat at his desk, and thought about the conversation he had with Jim: *Jim was mighty persistent that Albert and Mary resided right here in Fall City. Why would Joan tell him that they moved back here when they never did? Maybe they moved to another city and Jim got it mixed up with Fall City. According to Jim, Joan has called Fall City and talked to Albert and Mary. I wonder why Joan never called Dr. Wilborn or myself after she left. No one in Fall City has heard from her since she moved. Maybe she'll call when Jim gives her the message that he talked to me. On the other hand, Joan could be having hallucinations again; she might be sick. That might explain why she hasn't called me or anyone else in Fall City. She could have imagined that Albert and Mary moved back to Fall City and told Jim that. Maybe Joan needs to see Dr. Wilborn again.*

Sheriff McClotin leaned back in his chair and thought long and hard about the next decision he was about to make. Ten-minutes later, he picked up his phone and dialed Dr. Wilborn's office.

"Good morning, sheriff," Dr. Wilborn said after picking up his phone.

"Morning. Doc, I may have a problem," the sheriff said.

"What kind of problem?"

"Joan," Sheriff McClotin said.

"Joan ... which Joan? There are two that I can recall off the top of my head ... there's Joan Bellows and Joan Quinlin. Now, which one is it?"

"Neither one. The Joan I'm talking about is Joan Witherspoon."

"Oh, that Joan. Since she moved to Baltimore, I haven't heard from her. Have you heard from her? Is she doing okay?"

"I haven't heard from her either, and I don't know if she's doing okay," the sheriff said. "But she may be having those hallucinations again ... in Baltimore."

"If she hasn't contacted you, how do you know that she's having hallucinations?"

"Well, her boyfriend called me. He claims Joan told him that Albert and Mary moved back here years ago after leaving Baltimore. He also claims that Joan calls here to Fall City and talks to Albert and Mary. She just may be ill again, because Albert and Mary never moved back here," Sheriff McClotin said.

"I thought they lived with Joan in Baltimore?"

"I thought they lived with Joan in Baltimore too, but Albert and Mary supposedly moved back here after living in Baltimore for a couple of months. Joan's boyfriend said Joan drove them to a Baltimore bus station the day they left," the sheriff said.

"So you think Joan is having hallucinations again and her boyfriend has fallen prey to her illusions? In other words, he believes that Albert and Mary reside right here in Fall City because Joan has told him so?" Dr. Wilborn said.

"Yes. And who knows what else Joan may have told him. I remember you distinctly telling me about her hallucinations years ago. I'm concerned that Joan may hurt herself or someone else. Maybe—"

"Oh my God!" Dr. Wilborn said, cutting off Sheriff McClotin.

Sheriff McClotin was startled and said, "What's the matter, Doc?"

"You won't believe this, but Edith came to me on the morning after Joan, Mary, and Albert moved and mentioned something I thought was odd."

"Odd?" Sheriff McClotin said.

"I know I should have told you about this when it happened, but I didn't think anything of it. I pray to God we don't find anything."

"Tell me what? Find anything? Doc, you've got my head spinning. I'm totally confused now. What's going on?" Sheriff McClotin asked.

"Edith said she watched Joan drive down the dirt road leading away from her home, but then Joan's car suddenly stopped alongside the lake. That's when Edith thought Joan had forgotten something and probably was going to turn around and go back to the house. You see, Edith was happy because she assumed she would get a chance to say good-bye to Joan before she took off again. So Edith immediately started riding her bike toward the car, but she stopped when she saw Joan get out of the car, open the driver-side back door, and drag something out."

"Drag something out?" Sheriff McClotin said.

"Yes, but keep in mind that it was dark when Edith saw this."

"So what's she claiming she saw?" Sheriff McClotin asked.

"Edith said she saw Joan drag out two duffel bags."

"Two duffel bags ... so what is the big deal?" Sheriff McClotin said.

"I'm not quite sure what the big deal is just yet. It was dark and Edith could hardly see. All she knows is that both items were large and had the shape of duffel bags. She went on to say that Joan dumped those duffel bag shaped items into the lake and drove off without ever noticing that Edith was thirty or so yards behind her when this occurred."

"Doc, I understand why you didn't tell me about the duffel bag incident the first time, because Edith is always snooping around and getting into trouble. Besides, it wasn't any reason for you to be suspicious of Joan. But I'm curious—why are you worried about it now?"

"Because Albert and Mary have been gone for four years now and the last person to see or hear from them was probably Joan. I'm not quite sure what to think about the duffel bags. Who knows what those duffel bags could have been filled with ... trash, old clothes? Hell, Edith might have thought she saw two duffel bags ... she really can't say what was dumped into that lake. Right now I'm more concerned that Joan is probably having hallucinations again. She could be in dire need of medical assistance. Especially after she told her boyfriend that Albert and Mary live here."

"Joan might need medical attention," Sheriff McClotin said.

"It's a real possibility that she does, but what if Albert and Mary never left Fall City?"

"Never left! What are you getting at? They've been gone for four years now, and they haven't returned to Fall City." Sheriff McClotin said.

"What I mean is that they've been missing for four years but not gone. I believe they're still here. I believe that they are at the bottom of that lake. I believe those two duffel bags that Edith saw Joan put into that lake had Albert and Mary in them."

The sheriff shook his head. "Are you nuts? For all we know, those duffel bags could have been two large trash bags. Albert and Mary stuffed in duffel bags ... give me a break. Remember ... it was dark, and Edith might have thought she saw two duffel bag shaped objects. I just don't believe she saw what she claims she saw."

"Well, there is only one way to find out ... and that's to go down to that lake and see," Dr. Wilborn said.

Sheriff McClotin paused for a moment. He couldn't imagine Joan killing Albert and Mary, putting them into duffel bags, and then tossing them into that lake. He wanted to tell the doc to just forget the whole thing. He thought the whole idea of searching the lake for two duffel bags was crazy. He thought about it for a minute more and then reluctantly said, "I'll call Phil and have him contact Fred and Larry—our firefighting crew. Thank goodness Fred has scuba diving gear that he uses from time to time. I'll tell Phil to have them meet us at the lake with the scuba gear in about thirty-five-minutes. I'll come right over and pick you up."

"Okay," Dr. Wilborn said before hanging up.

23

It was ten o'clock on Saturday morning, and Robert was sitting at his kitchen table, drinking a beer. Cindy was still asleep when Robert decided to get up and drink himself into a stupor. He wanted to save his marriage, but he didn't know how, so he tried to ease the pain and grief by consuming alcohol. After his second beer, he poured himself a glass of rum and drank it straight. He just couldn't take Cindy's rejection of him while he was sober, so he started to get intoxicated to avoid the hurt. It really bothered Robert every time she shunned him, ignored him, or was just unresponsive to him—especially during sex. Today was the day that Robert planned to talk to Cindy about their marriage.

At ten-twenty-five, Cindy awoke, strolled into the kitchen without saying a word, opened up the refrigerator, and removed a stick of butter and a loaf of bread. She placed the loaf of bread and butter down on the kitchen table and removed two slices of bread. All the time, she never acknowledged that Robert was sitting there. Cindy dropped the slices of bread into the toaster and waited for them to brown. Thirty seconds later, the bread popped up from the toaster and she spread butter across both slices with a butter knife. Robert couldn't take the silence any longer, so he quickly stood up, holding on to his chair to balance himself, walked over to Cindy, grabbed her wrist, and said, "First of all, good morning. You used to say good morning to me all the time, but that changed for some reason."

Cindy broke loose from his grip and aimed the butter knife at Robert as if she were trying to defend herself. Robert was a bit too tipsy to notice Cindy was in a defensive posture.

"Cindy, could you please have a seat, because I have to ask you something," Robert said.

Cindy relaxed a little, placed the butter knife and toasted bread down on the kitchen table, and took a seat while Robert sat back down directly across from her.

Cindy frowned and said, "Good morning. What do you want to ask me?"

Robert grew nervous and almost forgot what he was going to say. He wanted to jump out of his chair, run to their liquor cabinet, grab the bottle of rum, and take a few quick swigs from it before saying anything else, but his knees were shaking so much he couldn't stand up to get to the liquor cabinet.

All he could do was look Cindy in her eyes and say, "Why do you hate me so much? I love you, but you don't love me. You're not affectionate toward me anymore. You don't talk to me. You just ignore me when I try to talk to you. I want to know what I can do to make our marriage work. I want my old Cindy back—the Cindy who loved me unconditionally. I want that Cindy who hugged and kissed me all the time and said nice things to me."

Cindy looked at the two empty bottles of beer and the empty glass that smelled of rum, all of which were sitting on the kitchen table, and said, "Robert, you have to be to work at noon today. I can't believe you sat here and drank those beers and rum knowing you have to go to work. I can smell the rum on your breath. I'm going to fix you some coffee to help sober you up before you go to work. You can't possibly drive in your condition. If they smell alcohol on your breath while you're at work, you could be fired."

Robert smiled and said, "You do care about me ... about my welfare. Thank you Cindy. Before you make the coffee, could you please tell me why you've been treating me so badly?"

Cindy lowered her head and said, "I don't mean to treat you badly, but I have a bipolar disorder. I've been in counseling for this problem. My therapist and doctor are helping me to cope with my bipolar condition. I'm supposed to take olanzapine, but I want to make a few more visits to my doctor to see if I can cure this disease without the help from olanzapine. I'm sorry I didn't tell you about this."

Cindy stood up, walked over to Robert, and hugged him. He was surprised and at a loss for words. After kissing Cindy on her cheek, he said,

"You should have told me. I want to help. I want to be a part of your life. What can I do to help?"

"I didn't tell you because I didn't want you to worry. You can help by being patient with me. My bipolar illness, called manic-depressive disorder, causes me to have mood swings. I can be very depressed at times and sometimes very euphoric. When I become depressed, I feel sad, lazy, or hopeless and lose interest or pleasure in most activities. When my mood shifts in the other direction, I feel full of energy. Sometimes my bipolar disorder causes me to have symptoms of depression and euphoria at the same time. It could cause me to make very poor choices or decisions without careful consideration. That's why I've been acting peculiar toward you. Now you know why I'm not talking to you or showing any type of affection! This may go on for a couple of months, but my doctor promised I will improve as time goes on, as long as I continue to undergo therapy and take the medicines prescribed. As I mentioned before, I would prefer not to take the olanzapine."

"Please forgive me for getting a little drunk before going to work. I got upset that you weren't talking to me. Now that I know you're fighting this bipolar disorder, I'll stop drinking," Robert said.

"Robert ... I forgive you. Don't you worry about anything. In a few months, I'll be back to my regular self and everything will be okay. Just go take a shower and come back down here and drink plenty of coffee. I'll even drive you to work. I'll have your lunch ready for you too."

Robert smiled, wobbled a little as he stood up, and went back to their bedroom to prepare for his shower.

Cindy watched Robert gleefully amble into their bedroom wearing a big smile. He was joyful, like a child who was on his way to Disneyland. Cindy took in a deep breath, exhaled, and wondered how long she could continue to lie to him about her fake bipolar sickness. She had to continue to act as if she really had this disease right up until the time when she moved out. On that day, she would tell Robert that it was all over. That day was getting closer and closer.

24

Joan was returning home from the local Farm Fresh grocery store when she decided to drive by Cindy and Robert's house. She was hoping she would catch Cindy at home, because she was bored and wanted to talk to her. Joan turned onto Cindy's street and was driving toward her home when she saw something unusual. Cindy was hugging a rather tall, good-looking man as they stood next to a sky-blue Lexus. Joan was three to four houses away from Cindy's home when she witnessed this act. Cindy smiled after hugging this man, and then he got into the Lexus and drove away. Cindy quickly dashed toward her home, unlocked her front door, and entered without ever noticing Joan as she drove by. Instead of stopping and visiting Cindy, Joan sped up and kept on driving, going right by Cindy's home. Joan was a little puzzled by Cindy's actions and was considering asking her who the mystery man was the next time they talked, but she decided not to. Joan didn't want to ruin their friendship by prying into Cindy's business.

25

Cindy drove into the parking garage, parked, and quickly made her way toward the elevator. She took the elevator up to the sixth floor, exited, and walked toward room 613. Halfway to the room, Cindy stopped and almost decided to go back, but she changed her mind and continued to the room. She started to have guilty feelings about what she was doing. She knew she was causing indecision, confusion, and deep grief for herself and her lover by meeting incognito like this. As their secret meetings continued, they both were falling more and more in love with each other. The whole world seemed to come to a complete stop when they were together. Nothing was more important to them than themselves. All prior engagements, plans, and appointments were thrown out the window when those two got the urge to see one another.

As Cindy neared room 613, she opened her purse and removed the key card. She inserted the card into the door slot, removed the card, turned the doorknob, and entered. She was all alone. Her lover hadn't arrived yet, so she took a shower, rubbed scented lotion all over her body, and sprawled out across the hotel bed naked. Fifteen-minutes elapsed before the hotel room door opened and Cindy's lover walked in. Cindy stood up and quickly embraced and passionately kissed her lover. Cindy could feel the warmth of her lover's hands firmly grasp her buttocks. Once Cindy's lover's clothes were removed, they both fell onto the bed and started to make love.

26

As Jim drove toward Joan's condominium, he didn't know what to do. Joan's birthday was seven days away, and he hadn't made contact with Albert and Mary yet. He was still unsure on how to acquire the phone number from Joan to call Albert and Mary. Maybe the sheriff in Fall City had it wrong. Maybe Albert and Mary were there but he wasn't aware of it.

Jim wasn't about to doubt Joan's words over some small-town sheriff's word. Why would Joan lie about something like that? It didn't make any sense. Jim had witnessed Joan call Albert and Mary on numerous occasions.

Jim pulled into Joan's driveway, parked, and got out. As he walked towards Joan's front door he was still confused about Albert and Mary's whereabouts. He opened Joan's front door with his key, entered, and instantly heard Joan talking to her puffer fish from her living room.

"Joan," Jim yelled out as he walked down her hallway and into the living room.

Joan turned away from her fish, walked toward Jim, gave him a hug, and said, "I'm glad you came by. I was about to feed my fish."

Jim kissed Joan on her forehead just before she left for the kitchen to retrieve her fish food. Joan grabbed her fish food, walked back into the living room, and started pouring the fish food into the tank.

Jim sat down on the couch, turned on the TV, and waited for Joan to join him. After feeding her fish, Joan cuddled up next to Jim and said, "I know that I must sound like a broken record at times, but I can't stop thinking about the two of us getting married. I love you, Jim, and I know that you love me. So we will be getting married about twelve months from now ... right?"

Jim looked her in the eyes and said, "Yes, we sure are baby."

She was holding out hope that Jim would say, *I've changed my mind, baby; let's get married as soon as possible!*

She felt hurt, confused, and upset that Jim wanted to wait so long before tying the knot. She had foolishly bought up the subject of marriage again to see if she would get a different answer, but it was the same answer as always ... *No—we have to wait one more year!* If Joan had heard the right answer, she would have broken off her illicit love affair and devoted all her love to Jim, but that wasn't the case.

Joan turned toward Jim and said, "I fully understand your position, and I respect you for it. Maybe you'll change your mind and ask for my hand in marriage way before our one-year deadline is up."

Jim kissed her on her cheek and said, “I know it will happen, but not for a few more months. You are the only person I want to marry. You just have to be patient with me.”

Joan smiled, stood up, and walked into the kitchen to make herself a drink while Jim watched TV. Joan retrieved a bottle of Crown Royal, a can of Pepsi, and a glass. After pouring some Pepsi and Crown Royal into her glass, she sat down at her kitchen table and thought about the mess she had created.

“Hey, Joan. Have you heard from Albert and Mary lately?” Jim bellowed out from the living room.

Joan took a couple sips of her drink and said, “I sure did. They called me last night and told me that they were doing fine and couldn’t wait to meet you when we visit them during our vacation.”

“Great. How long do you think it would take us to drive from here to Fall City?” Jim asked.

“Hmm ... maybe about five hours.”

“Hey, call Albert up and let me get the directions from him,” Jim said.

“Get directions! I know how to get there. Remember, I used to live there.”

“I know that, but I still want to talk to Albert,” Jim said.

“Right now?” Joan said before taking another sip of her drink.

“Yes, right now.”

“Oh ... okay. Give me about ten-minutes, and I’ll call them and let you talk to Albert,” Joan said.

A tremendous burden and sense of doubt was lifted off of Jim's shoulders after Joan promised to let him talk to Albert. He felt ashamed of himself for ever doubting or disbelieving Joan. Jim smiled and thought to himself: *Albert and Mary really do live in Fall City*.

Joan had finished her drink, ten-minutes later, walked into the living room and picked up the telephone. Jim scooted up to the edge of the couch and waited for Joan to make the call.

Joan dialed the number to Albert and Mary's house, put the phone on speaker, and set it back in its cradle. She turned the volume up so Jim could hear Albert's and Mary's voices. On the third ring, Joan said, "They're not home."

Just as Joan was about to depress the speaker button and cut off the phone, Mary picked up her phone and said, "Hello."

"Hi, Mary, this is Joan."

"Hey, Joan. How are you doing?"

"I'm doing fine. You know Jim and I are planning to visit you and Albert real soon," Joan said.

"Yes, we know. We chatted about that the last time you and I talked. You just let us know when you and Jim are coming, and we'll prepare our guest room for the both of you."

"I'll be sure to let you know. Oh, is Albert available to talk to Jim?"

"No, he's not. He went into town about thirty-minutes ago. He should be back later."

Jim interrupted and said, "Hi, Mary, I'm Jim. I can talk to you since Albert isn't home. By the way, it's a pleasure talking to you for the very first time. I can't wait to come to Fall City to meet you and Albert."

"I can't wait to meet you. I really shouldn't say this, but Joan can't stop talking about you when she calls us."

"I hope she's saying good things about me," Jim said.

"Not one bad word is ever said about you; she really loves you," Mary said.

Joan blushed and said, "Mary, I think Jim knows how much I love him."

Jim smiled and said, "Joan, can I talk to Mary in private? It's very important that I talk to her. Joan, believe me, it has nothing to do with you. Can you please go into the bedroom until I finish talking to her?"

Joan looked a little surprised by Jim's request, but she agreed, handed him the phone, and turned off the speakerphone. Joan went into her bedroom while Jim talked to Mary.

Jim finally got the opportunity to explain to Mary that he would like her and Albert to show up for Joan's surprise birthday party. But sadly Mary informed him that they wouldn't be able to make it because of prior commitments. Jim was extremely disappointed, but he explained to Mary that he and Joan would be coming to Fall City to visit them soon. After hanging up the phone, he somberly called for Joan to come back into the living room.

Jim hugged Joan, kissed her on her forehead,

and said, "I enjoyed talking to Mary. I can't wait until we visit them."

Joan smiled and said, "Too bad Albert wasn't home. He's a fantastic guy. Hey, why didn't you want me to hear your conversation?"

"That's my secret. Besides, you'll know in due time," Jim said.

"Oh, I hope it's something good."

"Believe me ... it isn't anything to worry about. You'll have a good laugh about it later."

Jim knew that he could trust Joan with all his heart now. He would never doubt her word again. Albert and Mary really did live in Fall City, South Carolina. That sheriff didn't know what he was talking about.

They sat down on the couch and started to watch TV together. Jim had a smile on his face like never before. He really seemed happy. He wasn't at all upset that Albert and Mary couldn't make it to Joan's surprise birthday party. On the contrary, he was overjoyed because he finally got to speak to Mary. He looked into Joan's eyes and said, "I love you and really trust you."

Joan lay her head down across Jim's lap and winced at the thought that Jim trusted her. She felt sick to her stomach. So far she had been successful in covering up her illicit love affair, but she was dreading the day when she would have to leave Jim.

27

Dr. Wilborn and Sheriff McClotin stood alongside the road parallel to the lake, watching Deputy Phil Goony assist Fred Ames and Larry Rawlings. Fred Ames and Larry Rawlings were volunteer firefighters for the Fall City Fire Department. Phil, Fred, and Larry were working together to search the lake for the two duffel bags. This lake was thirty-feet-deep, sixty-yards-long, and forty-five-yards wide. Fred put on his scuba gear, readied his waterproof flashlight, and slowly walked into the lake.

Fred disappeared from sight within a few seconds. Three-minutes later, his flashlight exposed two duffel bags at the bottom of the lake, not far from the road. He brought the first bag up from the bottom of the lake, and Larry and Phil dragged it out of the water and placed it on the side of the road near Dr. Wilborn and Sheriff McClotin. Ten-minutes later, the second duffel bag was placed next to the first one. Each duffel bag had a combination lock securing it.

"Well, it's time we open up these duffel bags and see what's in them," Sheriff McClotin said as everyone gathered around the duffel bags.

"I'll get the bolt cutters," Phil said before walking toward the cruiser.

Phil removed a bolt cutter from the trunk of his cruiser and cut the lock off of the first duffel bag. He placed the bolt cutter on the ground, looked at everyone, and then opened the duffel bag.

Phil looked into the bag, strained his eyes, and said, "Oh my God ... there's a body in here!"

Dr. Wilborn, the sheriff, and both firemen moved closer and peered into the bag. The sheriff couldn't believe his eyes. It was a body, all right, but whose? He could make out a skull with very fine strands of hair still attached, and some facial skin, but something was very peculiar. The bottom of the corpses feet were facing upwards. Both feet were protruding up-right ... positioned right next to the skull. The feet were shoeless, but oddly enough they had socks on.

The sheriff looked at Dr. Wilborn and both firemen and said, "It's a body all right, but it looks a little mangled! Phil, cut the lock on the other duffel bag."

Phil grabbed his bolt cutter, cut the lock, and opened the duffel bag only to discover a body in that bag too. The body was in the same position as the first one. The feet were protruding up-right next to its skull. This cadaver was shoeless but had socks on also, just like the other one. Both bodies were in such bad condition that they couldn't tell if they were male or female, young or old. Both of them had clothes on, but their clothes were rotted and indiscernible.

"Sheriff, you have to call the police in Durham. In all my years of practicing medicine, I've never seen bodies in such horrible condition. I wouldn't know where to begin. I think their legs were cut off in order to fit their bodies into these duffel bags. The only real way to know how they died is to have a medical examiner look them over. We're going to need the Durham police to handle this one," Dr. Wilborn said.

"I'll give them a call," Sheriff McClotin said. "This is terrible. Who would do something like this, and who are these two people?"

Dr. Wilborn leaned close to Sheriff McClotin and whispered, "Edith was right about seeing duffel bags being thrown into the lake. I'm no soothsayer, but I'll bet you anything that those two bodies are probably Albert and Mary Niphon."

Sheriff McClotin frowned, hesitated for a moment, and then hurried over to his cruiser and used the police radio to contact Ruth. He told her to call the state police in Durham, North Carolina, right away.

28

Jim was seated at the break room table, eating lunch, when his thoughts went back to the conversation he had with Sheriff McClotin. He was still upset that Sheriff McClotin wasn't aware that Albert and Mary actually lived in Fall City. Jim had planned on calling the sheriff back, to let him know that Albert and Mary did live there, but Joan had convinced him not to. They'd decided to inform the sheriff when they arrived in Fall City to visit Albert and Mary.

"Hey, Jim, you look a little puzzled. Are you okay?" Nelly said after entering the break room, interrupting Jim's thoughts.

"Oh ... hey, Nelly. I'm okay. I was just thinking about something, but it's not important. By the way, what did our manager, Francis, have you do today?"

Nelly placed his lunch bag down on the table, removed his bowl of spaghetti and meatballs, and placed it in the microwave. He set the timer for three-minutes after closing the microwave door and said, "Frances had me deliver the express mail, deliver six rather large packages for route ten, and case up all the mail on route thirty-three. After lunch I'm going to help Richard deliver mail to a couple of his apartment complexes. What did Francis have you do?"

Jim took a quick swig of his green tea and said, "He had me take a tray of letter mail to the Park View and Oak Town stations. Their mail was delivered to our station by mistake again. That has been happening quite a bit lately. Francis also asked me to drop off some paperwork to the postmaster. As soon as I finish my lunch, I'll be delivering mail to all of the businesses on route sixteen. After that I'll be delivering mail to the apartments on my route."

The microwave beeped, and Nelly removed his lunch. He sat down next to Jim and scooped up a spoonful of spaghetti and meatballs before saying, "How did Francis ever make manager and get assigned to our station? He's one of the worst managers that I've ever worked for. Hell, he's probably the worst manager in the whole city of Baltimore."

Jim laughed and said, "I don't know how he became a manager. It was either divine intervention or the postmaster loved him."

Nelly quickly gulped down his spoonful of spaghetti and meatballs before saying, "Both of those things had to have happen for Mr. Francis Sterdly to become a manager. Please, let's not talk about Sterdly anymore; I'm trying to enjoy my lunch."

"Sorry about that," Jim responded.

"Oh, I almost forgot ... I also have to take mail to four different carriers. I'll have to load up four heavy trays of mail and a bunch of parcels into my truck. Lifting those heavy trays of mail every day is killing me. My lower back, knees, and feet are always aching."

Jim patted Nelly on his back and said, "Take your time and eat. You have a whole thirty-minutes to relax, let your pain dissipate, and enjoy your lunch before you run that mail out to those carriers."

Nelly smiled and said, "Sometimes I only take twenty-minutes or less for lunch. And I almost never take my ten-minute break. I know that sounds crazy, but I'll probably do the same thing today so I can get that mail out to those carriers. The sooner I get that mail to them—the quicker they can finish delivering their mail."

"You aren't the only one who takes a shortened lunch break or skips his ten-minute break. I know a couple of carriers who never take their lunch break. They just run, run, run. You can see them driving in their mail trucks eating a sandwich or chomping down on a 7-Eleven hot dog. Some eat while they're delivering their mail—sandwich, candy bars, potato chips, and soda all stuck in their satchel along with their mail."

"It's what the postal service has come to," Nelly said. "The delivery of the mail comes first, no matter what the situation is. You may be sick, injured, tired, or even hungry, but you can't stop, because the mail has to be delivered. Some carriers, foolishly, have even thrown away mail because they don't have time to deliver it. What idiots!"

“If you don’t have time to deliver the mail, call and ask for help. You just can’t throw the mail away. The people who do that are crazy and doomed to be fired, and they could possibly serve jail time. The postal service has enough problems. Do you happen to know what those other problems are?” Jim asked.

“No ... what?”

“Well, where shall I start? The main problems are those managers and supervisors who may have no sense, or idea, of how long it takes to deliver mail for various routes. Some don’t factor in the weather, how late you leave the office, or how heavy the mail is; they just want you back in the station in eight hours! Those managers and supervisors attend the postmaster meetings, drink the Kool-Aid, and become yes men. Before they go into these meetings, some of those supervisors and managers are human. In other words, they have some sympathy and understanding of what the carriers are going through. They actually try to help the carriers, but after a few of those Kool-Aid-drinking meetings with the postmaster, they become complete zombies—robots. And they lose what common sense they have. At that point they are brainwashed and they start running the carriers and clerks into the ground.”

“I agree with you, but some don’t fall for that Kool-Aid. Many hold onto their integrity and use common sense.”

“You’re right, but most managers and supervisors are spineless wimps,” Jim replied.

"Jim, we could talk all day about how screwed up management is, but we only have thirty-minutes for lunch," Nelly said just before scooping up another spoonful of his spaghetti and meatballs.

"Go ahead and enjoy your meal. I'll see you later. I'm going to deliver the mail to the businesses on route sixteen," Jim said before gathering up his lunch items and leaving the break room.

Nelly waved good-bye and then quickly stuffed more food into his mouth. He was rushing to finish his lunch so he could hurry up and get the mail to the carriers. Ten- minutes later, he finished eating his food and was ready to go. He had become accustomed to indigestion.

29

Dr. Henry Koski, medical examiner, threw on his full-length smock, put on his latex gloves, moved to the table where the bodies lay, and adjusted the microphone hanging from the ceiling directly above him. Before starting, Dr. Koski glanced over at Dr. Wilborn, Sheriff McClotin, and Durham Police Department Detective Josh Sanders. All three were standing motionless and very quiet near the entrance to the morgue. Dr. Koski was sanctioned by the US District Court of North Carolina to perform a medical-legal autopsy on the bodies found in the duffel bags and render a decision on the causes of death. The Durham Police Department had sent one of their ambulances to Fall City to pick up the two bodies and bring them back to Durham for Dr. Koski to perform his autopsy. Sheriff McClotin used his patrol car, and he and Dr. Wilborn followed the ambulance to Durham in hopes of discovering who those poor souls were ... and what caused their terrible deaths.

Dr. Koski stood close to the bodies, cleared his throat, and started talking into the microphone:

"All x-rays, photographs, and weight and measurements of victims were recorded earlier. Both bodies were found to be badly decomposed. Being submerged in water for over four years has caused massive deterioration. Of note ... both corpses had no fingertips, their legs were cut off, and their teeth were missing. No identification was found on either victim."

Dr. Koski stopped talking and edged closer to the bodies.

Sheriff McClotin felt a rush of heat to his face after hearing about the fingertips and teeth being missing from the bodies. With no identification, it would be next to impossible to identify these people without their teeth or fingerprints.

Dr. Koski revealed a scalpel and used it to make his thoracic abdominal incision into the first corpse. His incision was made from shoulder to shoulder, across the chest, and midline to the pubic area. This was referred to as the Y incision. After exposing the heart and lungs using his rib cutter, Dr. Koski removed what blood he could from the various internal organs. The lungs, esophagus, trachea, and heart were all removed and examined. Contents of the stomach were measured and prepared for toxicology tests. Lastly, Dr. Koski used his bone saw to cut out the front quadrant of the skull. After removing that bony part of the skull, he removed the brain for examination.

During this two-hour examination of the first corpse, Dr. Wilborn and Sheriff McClotin became very much acquainted with Detective

Sanders. While Dr. Koski was performing the autopsy, they made themselves some coffee, removed three chairs from the hospital cafeteria, and carried the chairs and coffee back into the examination area of the morgue, where they sat down and continued to watch Dr. Koski perform his ghastly duties.

At the end of the two-hour examination, Dr. Koski used his Hagedorn needle to sew up the first corpse, removed his surgical mask and gloves, and said, "Gentlemen, I suggest you all retire for the night. I plan on having some late dinner and then return here to perform my next autopsy on the second corpse; that will probably take me another two-hours. Once I've completed that final autopsy and all the medical tests, I'll have the cause of death for both of these bodies shortly. The one thing that I'm quite sure about right now is that each of these individuals died a horrible death. As I said earlier, their fingertips were removed, their legs were cut off, and all their teeth were extracted. They were both brutally butchered. It's a possibility that they may have been somehow rendered unconscious or dead before having their teeth, legs, and fingertips removed. I would certainly hope that that was the case, because what happened to them was extremely painful. So far it doesn't look as though I may be able to identify them."

Dr. Wilborn pulled out his wallet, removed a small picture and said, "Dr. Koski, we really appreciate your help concerning this case. For what it's worth, Sheriff McClotin and I have a photo of the people we believe were murdered. They were a couple by the name of Albert and Mary Niphon."

"Detective Sanders may be interested in seeing that photo. Gentlemen, I'm going to have some dinner now," Dr. Koski said before removing his smock and leaving the examination room.

Dr. Wilborn turned toward Detective Sanders and said, "Here is a picture of Albert and Mary Niphon walking toward the entrance of my office. This was the very first day they moved into Fall City about thirteen-years ago. All newcomers who move into our town must make a visit to my office, get their picture taken, and collect a welcome-aboard package consisting of a ham, fruits, and candy—and meet some of the citizens. I clearly remembered that day because they were very upset when I took their picture, but they soon calmed down after realizing that it was a Fall City tradition."

Detective Sanders took the picture and stared at the individuals. He rubbed his chin, looked at Dr. Wilborn, and said, "Albert and Mary Niphon. These faces look familiar, but the names don't ring a bell."

"I'm guessing Albert and Mary are probably in their late sixties now ... that's if they're still alive. Albert was about five feet eleven inches tall and always kept his wavy salt-and-pepper hair short. Albert had a cheerful and bubbly personality and always wore a two-piece suit. Mary had long mercury-red hair down to her shoulders. She was a couple inches shorter than Albert. She always wore pant suits. Her ladylike personality was infectious; everyone enjoyed being around her. They were good friends of ours. We believe that they're the ones on that table," Sheriff McClotin said.

As the sheriff looked on, he had a heartfelt flashback of their past years as residents of Fall City: *When they first came to Fall City, Albert went to work as a third-grade teacher at Roberson's Elementary School. All the parents and their eight-year-old kids loved him. Albert made sure that he stayed after school, when needed, to help all his students with homework and projects. He even invited the students and their parents to come to school over the weekends to get help if needed. He was teacher of the year for eight of the thirteen-years he worked there. He retired a year before Joan graduated college. That was a big loss for Roberson's Elementary School. Mary worked part-time at the bowling alley and movie theater as the assistant manager. The teenagers couldn't wait until Friday night to go to the bowling alley, because they knew Mary would provide them with one small bag of popcorn and a small Coca-Cola for free. Mary, on Saturday evenings, would always provide the teenagers with the same items at the movie theater. The kids loved it, and so did management. That free popcorn and soda brought more kids into both the bowling alley and movie theater every time. Those teenagers almost always purchased extra items, which raised the concessions sales. Over the months, Mary became a favorite among the children and teenagers. Mary had retired at the same time that Albert had to the disappointment of the children and parents of Fall City.*

"Detective Sanders, you said their faces look familiar to you. Do you think you might have known Albert and Mary?" Dr. Wilborn asked.

Detective Sanders paused for a moment and said, "If my memory serves me correctly, I believe I know these two individuals. They very much resemble two people I arrested a long time ago. It was some fifteen-years ago that I arrested them for stealing a baby from one of our hospitals. They never really cooperated with the authorities after that arrest ... they just disappeared. But there is one problem: their names were not Albert and Mary Niphon during that time."

Dr. Wilborn and Sheriff McClotin both had looks of shock on their faces after hearing what Detective Sanders had said.

"Are you sure it was Albert and Mary Niphon?" Sheriff McClotin asked. "They were two of our most upstanding citizens."

"They were good people. It must be a mistake," Dr. Wilborn said.

"I could be wrong, but I think I still have DNA and pictures of these two people. I'm sure they changed their names to Albert and Mary Niphon to avoid the police. I will have Dr. Koski take DNA samples from both corpses and compare them to the DNA that I have. Meanwhile, I will search through my database and files to see if these are the same two people that I busted years ago. I have their names on the tip of my tongue, but I just can't remember right now."

"You have the DNA of Albert and Mary?" Dr. Wilborn asked.

"Yes. It all started when a baby boy was stolen from Southside Hospital here in Durham. Neighbors remembered Albert and Mary Niphon moving into a plush two-story home one afternoon, but there was one problem: Albert and Mary had moved into their home alone. There were no infants, teenagers, or other adults living with them. Oh, and Mary wasn't pregnant—neighbors swore to that! Two weeks after moving into their new home, they were seen carrying an infant around. At first the neighbors thought Albert and Mary were babysitting for neighbors or friends, but no one ever saw a baby being picked up or dropped off at Albert and Mary's home. This brought plenty of attention to Albert and Mary, because a baby boy was stolen from the Southside Hospital two weeks after Albert and Mary moved into their home. The baby Albert and Mary had, according to various witnesses, looked just like the infant that was nabbed from the hospital.

We immediately picked up Albert and Mary for questioning and took them and the infant to our police station. The biological parents of that infant, the Hudsons, and the nurses and doctor who cared for that infant were also there. Less than thirty seconds of observing the infant, the doctor and the nurses swore that this was the Hudsons' baby. And they claimed it was the baby stolen from the hospital. The Hudsons were elated, because they instantly recognized that this was their newborn baby. Albert and Mary immediately denied the accusations that they'd kidnapped the baby. They kept repeating that the baby was theirs, so I ordered parental testing for Albert, Mary, and the Hudsons to settle this problem. Three days later, the results of the test came back; they revealed that Albert and Mary were not the biological parents, but the Hudsons were. I arrested Albert and Mary and charged them with kidnapping."

Sheriff McClotin couldn't believe what he was hearing. He sat there in bewilderment. Dr. Wilborn looked at Sheriff McClotin and then Detective Sanders and said, "Albert and Mary were arrested and charged with kidnapping?"

"Detective Sanders, are you sure that the two people you arrested were Albert and Mary Niphon?" Sheriff McClotin asked.

"I'm not one-hundred-percent sure, but my gut is telling me that these are the same two felons I arrested years ago," Detective Sanders said. "Can I hold on to this picture?"

"You can have that picture," Dr. Wilborn replied. "This is so hard to believe. Can you tell us what eventually happened with Albert and Mary after you arrested them?"

"First of all, they both were very manipulative. They both needed to have a child, no matter what. Their warped minds and conniving personalities, coupled with the inability to have children of their own, forced them to steal that infant. After they were arrested, they went to court, where their defense lawyer pleaded for mercy and claimed they both had tried everything to have a child of their own. He said they had lost touch with reality and just cracked—flipped out. He went on to explain how they had tried for years to have kids and raise a family but couldn't. He cited some medical problem of Mary's that caused her to miscarry three times. He even explained the mental anguish they both endured when they couldn't have any kids. According to their lawyer, this caused them to act irrationally. He went on to say that this was their first crime and it wouldn't happen again because they were planning on adopting in the future. Unfortunately the judge believed every word their lawyer told him. The judge sentenced them both to twenty-four months of probation and a five-hundred-dollar fine. Their probation prohibited them from leaving the city of Durham for any reason without consulting their probation officer first. They served their first eighteen months of probation without a hitch, but then they just suddenly and unexpectedly disappeared one day, with only a few more months left to go on their probation. They vacated their home and left all their belongings behind—I mean everything. They just vanished. Of course, they violated their probation when they left the city. After that, we never found or heard from them again."

"This can't be the same Albert and Mary that came to our peaceful town. They practically raised Joan and let her live with them for a number of years before they moved to Baltimore with her," Dr. Wilborn said.

"They couldn't have done those things; they were great people," Sheriff McClotin said.

"I know all of this is hard to believe, but we will know for certain when I compare the DNA that I have with Dr. Koski's DNA. "I believe it's them; that's why they didn't want their pictures taken by you when they came to your office. I'm still trying to recall the names they went by when they were here, but I just can't remember. When I look at my records their names will be there."

"That's one way to get to the bottom of this," Dr. Wilborn said. "Well, it's no use hanging around here any longer. It will be some time before Dr. Koski comes back with a full report. Detective Sanders, could you please take us back to our hotel room?"

"Sure," Detective Sanders replied. "I can have that DNA result for you in a couple of days. With a little luck, we'll get to the bottom of this, and then we can concentrate on who murdered them."

Sheriff McClotin flinched a bit and wondered when to tell Detective Sanders that there is a suspect who may be responsible for the deaths of those two individuals.

"Yes ... we can concentrate on who murdered them," Sheriff McClotin faintly said, as if he'd lost his voice.

They all left the morgue, and Detective Sanders proceeded to drive Dr. Wilborn and Sheriff McClotin back to their hotel for the night.

30

"Hello," Dr. Wilborn said.

"Good morning, Dr. Wilborn. This is Detective Sanders. I have the results from the DNA."

"Good. Hold on one minute. I'm going to let the sheriff know and put you on speakerphone."

"Hey, sheriff, finish up in that bathroom. I've got Detective Sanders on speakerphone out here. He has the DNA results," Dr. Wilborn said.

Sheriff McClotin came rushing out of the bathroom and took a seat next to the phone.

"I'm sorry I didn't contact you or the sheriff during the past couple of days, but the DNA results finally came back. I received all the results this morning. Well now, the DNA for those two corpses, whom you call Albert and Mary Niphon, matches the DNA for Samuel and Sue Harrington. In other words, Albert and Mary Niphon are actually Samuel and Sue Harrington. They changed their names to Albert and Mary Niphon after they left Durham."

Dr. Wilborn didn't know what to say. He was stunned to hear that Albert and Mary were criminals and was saddened that they had officially been identified as the two corpses in the morgue. He was speechless for a moment but gathered his thoughts and finally said, "So it's true. They were the couple who kidnapped that baby and ended up on those slabs in the morgue."

"I'm afraid so. Now that we have identified who was killed, we need to find out who murdered them," Detective Sanders said.

"We may know who the alleged suspect is," Sheriff McClotin responded.

"What ... how do you know this?" Detective Sanders asked.

Sheriff McClotin nervously looked at Dr. Wilborn and then turned back toward the speakerphone before saying, "We've suspected someone for about a week now, but we were unsure if that person could have done this."

"Who is this person?" Detective Sanders asked.

Dr. Wilborn hesitated a moment and said, "Her name is Joan—Joan Witherspoon. She's about twenty-seven-years-old and lives in Baltimore, Maryland. Sheriff McClotin can get in touch with Joan because he has her boyfriend's phone number. I was told, some years ago, by Edith, one of our Fall City citizens, that she witnessed Joan dump two duffel bags into the lake. Those two duffel bags had Albert and Mary Nipon—aliases Samuel and Sue Harrington—in them."

"I have two questions for you: can you trust your witness? And, do you know Joan very well?" Detective Sanders asked.

"Edith can be trusted, and Joan was very close to the both of us," Dr. Wilborn said. "You see, Sheriff McClotin and I have known Joan for a very long time—as is the case with most of the young adults during our tenure in Fall City. It's hard to believe that Joan could have committed such a horrible crime."

"Well, the next step is to call the authorities in Baltimore to let them know about Joan," Detective Sanders said. "They must pick her up for questioning immediately. And you'll have to contact your witness and let her know that she'll have to testify to what she saw."

"I will contact Edith, our witness, when we get back to Fall City. We'll check out of this hotel and prepare to drive back within the hour," Sheriff McClotin said.

"Don't forget to contact the Baltimore Police Department about Joan," Detective Sanders replied.

"We'll do that. And, Sheriff McClotin will also contact Joan's boyfriend to get her address when we arrive in Fall City."

"I'll ask him for Joan's address for the purpose of visiting her," Sheriff McClotin said. "I don't want to let on that the police need her address to question her about a double murder. Once I have the address, I'll pass it on to the Baltimore Police and explain everything to them. I will provide them with your name and contact information, Detective Sanders, along with Dr. Koski's name and contact information. The police in Baltimore need to be in communication with the both of you before they talk to Joan."

"If needed ... Dr. Koski and I will be ready to travel to Baltimore when we receive the call from the Baltimore Police," Detective Sanders said. "We will make arrangements to bring the bodies along too."

"Okay," Sheriff McClotin replied. "We appreciate all your help, Detective Sanders. Dr. Wilborn and I will see you soon."

"Teamwork is vital when dealing with cases like this one. I'm looking forward to seeing you two again. Have a safe trip back to Fall City," Detective Sanders said.

"We'll be in touch," Dr. Wilborn said before hanging up the phone.

Prior to driving back to Fall City both Dr. Wilborn and Sheriff McClotin prayed that Joan had absolutely nothing to do with the murder of Albert and Mary Niphon ... alias Samuel and Sue Harrington.

31

When Dr. Wilborn and Sheriff McClotin returned to Fall City, they informed the entire town that Albert and Mary Niphon had been murdered. They explained that Sheriff McClotin, along with the Baltimore and Durham police departments, were working together to solve their murders. They explained that both of their bodies had been placed into duffel bags and dumped into the lake. They didn't explain the brutality of their murders; if there were any suspect or suspects, nor did they mention Albert and Mary's criminal past. The citizens of Fall City couldn't believe that they had been murdered. They all wondered who could have done such a ghastly thing.

Not long after the announcement that Albert and Mary Niphon had been murdered, somehow, word leaked out that Joan Witherspoon was a suspect in their murders. No one could believe that Joan had a murderous bone in her body. When the citizens of Fall City were told that Edith witnessed Joan dump those duffel bags into the lake, they called Edith senile, old, and as blind as a bat. Many of the citizens refused to believe that Edith saw anything resembling duffel bags during that obscure early morning hour—especially if she was thirty yards or more away. They believed Edith had made a horrible mistake. But Edith adamantly stood her ground against the angry crowd of citizens who thought she was loony, and she sternly repeated what she had witnessed. Edith never wavered from her testimony, and for that she was fast becoming the scourge of Fall City.

The following morning, after everyone had heard what Edith had said about Joan, Dr. Wilborn sat in his office and thought long and hard on what he was to do next. With the town in an uproar about Edith, he was about to start a firestorm of controversy. He picked up his phone and called Sheriff McClotin.

"Hello," Sheriff McClotin said.

"Sheriff, I don't know how to say this, but I believe Joan's parents may have been murdered. And, I'm trying to convince myself that Joan didn't do it!"

The sheriff almost dropped his phone. He took in a deep breath, exhaled, and said, "I think poor Joan has been accused of enough murders right now. She doesn't need to be blamed for her parents' deaths too. Besides, she hasn't been officially accused of murdering Albert and Mary."

"I know this sounds crazy, but something isn't right. Now that I think about it ... I may have signed off on Bill and Rachel's death certificates too soon. I put a medical condition down for the cause of Bill and Rachel's demise in my haste to help Joan get through what grief she may have experienced. My underlying cause of death for the both of them was a heart attack. I went on to say that the contributing factors to their deaths were chronic bronchitis caused from cigarette smoking, and probably overexertion. At that time I had no reason to believe that they were murdered. I may have been wrong about this whole thing. They could have been murdered!"

"Now, now Doc, I know you and I felt a little uneasy about Joan's reactions to her parents' deaths on that dreary day some years ago, but her lack of emotions shouldn't warrant a guilty verdict for murder. We both thought something was odd about her behavior, but certain people react differently from others when it comes to grieving for their loved ones."

"Sheriff, I agree with you about how people react differently, but I felt a little troubled that day. I feel even more perturbed now. Don't ask me why, but something is wrong. Even though Albert and Mary Niphon had a criminal past, they actually thought that Joan had murdered her parents. Maybe they were murdered because they found out that Joan killed her parents. I truly believe that Bill and Rachel's bodies must be exhumed in order for me to determine whether they died from heart attacks caused from chronic bronchitis or if they were murdered."

"Okay, I'll go along with whatever you think is right. Remember: we have a town mad with Edith right now for insinuating that Joan may have murdered Albert and Mary. Now you want to add in that Joan could've murdered her parents too! Can you imagine the reaction and shock from our citizens? We are looking at big trouble if you announce this."

"I'm totally confused right now. I don't know what to believe or do, but we can't tell anyone in Fall City the real reason why we are exhuming Bill and Rachel's bodies. If asked, we'll just tell them that we are relocating them to Baltimore to be near Joan."

"They may think it odd to do that, after so many years, but what else are we going to tell them?" Sheriff McClotin said.

"We'll explain that we are transporting their bodies to a gravesite near where Joan lives in Baltimore. Now that we've gotten that out of the way, can you put on your judge's hat and put together a court order to exhume Bill and Rachel's bodies for a forensic examination? Please include that this is in response to a criminal investigation because we believe that they may have been murdered. Let everyone involved know not to discuss this ordeal because it's an unsolved murder case. Also, we won't contact Joan about this, because she might refuse to have their bodies exhumed—for obvious reasons."

"Wait one minute. We should contact Detective Sanders and the Baltimore Police and ask them to hold off on questioning Joan until after we get Bill and Rachel's bodies exhumed and examined. I don't want them questioning her for the murders of Albert and Mary Niphon until we find out how Bill and Rachel died. It's best to present all the charges at once against her. That's if she's guilty of murdering anyone," Sheriff McClotin said.

"Agreed," Dr. Wilborn said.

Sheriff McClotin moaned and said, "I'll contact the Baltimore Police and Detective Sanders right away. I hope we're wrong about this. I hope we're wrong about Joan."

"I hope so too," Dr. Wilborn sadly responded.

32

A Durham Police Department forensic toxicologist performed the examination of Bill and Rachel at the Fall City morgue after they were exhumed from their Fall City gravesites. This toxicologist traveled from Durham to Fall City at the behest of Sheriff McClotin.

After the examination, a copy of the toxicologist's test results and summary were sent to the Baltimore Police Department, since Joan lived there, and a copy was provided to Sheriff McClotin.

Dr. Wilborn rushed over to Sheriff McClotin's office, where they both reviewed the toxicologist's results and analysis.

To the displeasure of both Sheriff McClotin and Dr. Wilborn, the test results revealed that lethal amounts of tetrodotoxin were found in both Bill and Rachel's bodies. The report's summary went on to explain that tetrodotoxin was a highly dangerous poison and that the source of this poison was from certain types of animals. The various fish that could have possibly carried this poison were trigger fish, ocean sunfish, porcupine fish, and puffer fish. Certain worms, a certain type of toad, a specific type of crab, and a few other rare animal species carried tetrodotoxin also. The summary went on to say that both victims had died a hideous death due to the intake or consumption of this poison. The toxicologist believed that the victims' first symptoms, prior to their deaths, would have been slight numbness of their lips, tongues, and skin. Additionally, they probably experienced excruciating headaches, and vomiting. Paralysis would have followed, limiting movement. Respiratory problems would have ensued, and their speech would even have been hampered. The toxicologist believed that their paralysis became worse and they both succumbed to heart attacks. They would have died within two-hours of consuming the tetrodotoxin.

Sheriff McClotin hadn't any idea how Bill and Rachel's bodies had been poisoned with tetrodotoxin. He was completely baffled by the results of the toxicologist's report—until he remembered Joan had owned puffer fish.

"Doc, Joan did own puffer fish. The only way for someone to have tetrodotoxin in their system ... is to have ingested it."

"We have to question Joan about this," Dr. Wilborn said. "First we need to ask her if puffer fish is something her parents normally ate. Joan will be free of any murder accusations, in my opinion, if she claims her parents willingly ate puffer fish. On the other hand, we have to find out how her parents died from tetrodotoxin if Joan claims that her parents never ate her puffer fish. There's a good chance that Joan didn't have anything to do with their demise."

"I totally agree with you ... there are people that consume puffer fish on a regular basis. I read some years ago that some of those same people have incorrectly prepared puffer fish for consumption and accidentally died. The gonads, liver, intestines, and skin of the puffer fish can contain extremely high amounts of tetrodotoxin. It's a possibility that Bill and Rachel inadvertently consumed those parts of the puffer fish."

"Well, Joan can't be guilty of murder if her parents misguidedly prepared those puffer fish for themselves. That would be considered accidental poisoning. Actually, I didn't even know people could eat puffer fish."

"Many people consider puffer fish a delicacy—especially the Japanese. Not too long ago there was a fatal poisoning from puffer fish in Fairfax County, Virginia. Two people fried their puffer fish and mistakenly ate the skin. They both died instantly from the heavy amounts of tetrodotoxin in the skin of that puffer fish. There are plenty of puffer fish in the mid-Atlantic coastal waters. People do eat those fish, but they can be highly toxic if you don't know what you're doing."

"That's horrible!" Dr. Wilborn said. "It's beginning to sound more and more like Joan's parents prepared their puffer fish wrong ... and paid with their lives. You'll have to contact the Baltimore Police Department and let them know that we're on our way to Baltimore and would like to question

Joan about the death of her parents and about the deaths of Albert and Mary Niphon too. Also, let Detective Sanders know that we have the toxicological results for Joan's parents."

"Before we go to Baltimore, we'd better have Edith provide us with a written statement," Sheriff McClotin said. "It should just state what she witnessed Joan do with those two duffel bags that contained the bodies of Albert and Mary Niphon. I'll have Edith come to my office at 8:00 a.m. tomorrow and provide us with that statement. I'll let Detective Sanders know to meet us at my office at 8:00 a.m. as well to be a witness to her testimony."

"Good idea. Get a good night's sleep, and I'll see you at your office tomorrow morning," Dr. Wilborn said before leaving Sheriff McClotin's office.

"Will do; we have a long day ahead of us tomorrow," Sheriff McClotin replied.

33

Sheriff McClotin, Dr. Wilborn, Detective Sanders, Edith, and Deputy Goony were all present at the sheriff's office at seven-fifty-five a.m. the following morning. They all sat down at the sheriff's conference table while Deputy Goony provided everyone with coffee and doughnuts. He also assured Edith that he would assist her in any way possible to ensure that she filled out her statement correctly.

Fifty-five-minutes later, with assistance from Deputy Goony, Edith had completed her written statement. Sheriff McClotin stood up, walked over to Edith, and said, "Edith, thank you so much for your statement. I realize you've been ridiculed by some of our citizens for speaking the truth about what you witnessed, but don't let that bother you. We really appreciate your courage and honesty concerning this case."

"You're welcome. I know people look down on me and consider me a nut, but they just don't know that I'm as friendly and honest as a person can be. I really don't care how they feel toward me, because I'm doing our community a service by helping you to solve the murders of Albert and Mary. I still don't want to believe that Joan had anything to do with the murders of Albert and Mary. Joan is such a kind and gentle person. Joan's parents, Bill and Rachel, raised Joan the right way and they were my closest friends. I miss them dearly. After my husband died, Bill and Rachel and I became really good friends. They would often invite me over for lunch, and they always asked me if I needed anything. They never paid any attention to the crazy talk about me. They just chuckled at all the complaints and innuendos directed at me. They were like family to me."

"Well, Edith, we have to drive to Baltimore this morning to provide the police with your statement and to question Joan about this whole ordeal," Dr. Wilborn said. "We don't want to keep you any longer."

"Yes, we have to get on the road," Sheriff McClotin said.

Edith stood up, grabbed Sheriff McClotin's arm, and said, "Joan couldn't have stuffed Albert and Mary into those duffel bags and put them into that lake. Yes, I did see Joan dragging those duffel bags from her car and rolling them right into that lake, but I just don't believe she killed them. Joan didn't kill them ... I know she didn't. Sheriff, is there a chance that those divers fished out the wrong duffel bags? Could there have been other duffel bags in that lake? Maybe the duffel bags that Joan dumped in the lake are still there."

"Edith, unfortunately, there were only two

duffel bags in that lake," Sheriff McClotin said. "We went back the following day and had the divers search the entire lake for additional evidence. No additional evidence—including other duffel bags—were found. We still can't believe that Joan could have done this. That's why Dr. Wilborn, Detective Sanders, and I must go to Baltimore to question Joan about the bodies in those duffel bags and about her puffer fish. We have to find out what happened."

Edith sat back down and said, "Puffer fish? What about her puffer fish?"

Dr. Wilborn looked at Sheriff McClotin, looked back at Edith, sighed, and said, "We'll fill you in about Joan's puffer fish at a later time."

Edith thought for a moment, rubbed her chin, and said, "I bet Albert and Mary had something to do with Joan's puffer fish."

Sheriff McClotin's body turned rigid. He cleared his throat and said, "Edith, what do Albert and Mary have to do with Joan's puffer fish?"

"I really don't know what they had to do with Joan's puffer fish, but I overheard them mention them," Edith replied.

"Can you tell us under what circumstance you heard Albert and Mary discuss Joan's puffer fish?" Dr. Wilborn asked.

Edith corrected her posture in the chair and said, "Well, it all started when I rode my bike over to Bill and Rachel's house about five p.m. just to say hi. That was in March ... the same day that Bill and Rachel were found dead. When I arrived, I placed my bike alongside Bill and Rachel's house under the canopy of one of their windows. That particular window was on the side of their house ... and I placed my bike there because it was raining. Normally, if it wasn't raining, I would've just ridden right up to their front door and rung their door bell. After parking my bike I walked toward the front of the house. And, just before I turned the corner, to go to their door and ring their doorbell, I heard this wicked laughter coming from Albert and Mary. That laughter made me stop before turning the corner. That laughter unnerved me so much that I decided to just peek around the corner to see what was going on. All the while, I stayed hidden from sight. As Albert and Mary were walking from Bill and Rachel's house toward their house, I heard Albert say, *'I sure hope they enjoy that puffer fish for dinner tonight.'* I immediately thought that they may have had dinner with Bill and Rachel. And, I assumed they probably ate a couple of Joan's puffer fish. But ... I also didn't believe that Bill and Rachel would've eaten Joan's puffer fish without Joan's permission. Besides, Joan wouldn't have liked that at all; she really loves her puffer fish. Just before Albert and Mary opened their front door to enter their house, they let out one more cackle of laughter. It sent chills up my spine. At that point I felt obligated to let Joan know that a couple of her puffer fish may have been eaten for dinner. Instead of knocking on Bill and Rachel's door, I went home. Later that evening, I rode back to Bill and Rachel's house to let Joan know about her puffer fish, but I forgot to tell her after I almost ran her over with my bike. I felt so bad and embarrassed for almost hitting Joan with my bike that I rode back home without ever telling her about her puffer fish."

There was complete silence in Sheriff's McClotin's office for a moment. No one knew what to say or do. The sheriff took a seat and said, "I believe they fed Joan's puffer fish to Bill and Rachel."

Dr. Wilborn pulled out a handkerchief from his back pocket, wiped the perspiration from his forehead, and said, "That explains where the tetrodotoxin came from. They fed Bill and Rachel puffer fish."

Edith was totally confused. She looked at Dr. Wilborn and said, "Tetro ... what?"

"Edith, I promise you we'll explain all of this very shortly," Dr. Wilborn replied.

Sheriff McClotin quickly glanced over at Deputy Goony and said, "Please prepare to have Edith write out another statement."

Edith looked confused after hearing that. Her eyebrows shot upward in surprise, and she said, "Sheriff, was something wrong with my first statement?"

Sheriff McClotin looked at Edith and said, "Your statement was fine. You didn't make any mistakes, but before we move on, we need to have your word that you won't let anyone in Fall City know what we talked about here today."

Edith took in a deep breath, blew it out, and

said, “You can trust me. I know how hush-hush police work can be. I won’t tell a soul about what we said here today.”

“Great,” Sheriff McClotin said. “Deputy Goony will have you write out another statement. Just write down everything you just told us starting with the laughter you heard coming from Albert and Mary. Just explain it as it happened ... just as you told us ... as you witnessed it.”

“I’m confused ... why would you want to know about some puffer fish being fed to Bill and Rachel? It isn’t a crime to feed fish to people,” Edith said with a perplexed expression.

“It’s not a crime to feed fish to anyone, but if that fish is poisonous, then it’s a crime,” Sheriff McClotin explained. “We know that Bill and Rachel were poisoned by tetrodotoxin. The puffer fish that they consumed contained a poisonous substance called tetrodotoxin, and they died from it. That was probably Joan’s puffer fish.”

Edith didn’t say a word. She looked dumbfounded and shocked. She looked over at Dr. Wilborn and then back at Sherriff McClotin before she started to cry.

Dr. Wilborn stood up and walked over to Edith. He handed her a box of tissues, patted her on her shoulders, and said, “Everything will be okay, Edith. This is complicated, but we need to know how Bill and Rachel got that poison into their systems. We’re as devastated as you are about this. With your testimony, we’ll prove that Joan didn’t murder her parents.”

Edith stopped crying, wiped her tears away with a tissue, and said, "Joan is being blamed for the murder of Bill and Rachel now? You mean to tell me that Bill and Rachel were poisoned by Joan's puffer fish? They didn't die of heart attacks? I should have said something to Joan as soon as she came home that evening from school, but I didn't. It was a cold, rainy night, and I almost ran her over with my bike. I should have stopped and told her what I heard Albert and Mary say that night. Maybe Joan and I could have saved her parents' lives. Joan is innocent ... Albert and Mary killed her parents."

Sheriff McClotin looked Edith in her eyes and said, "Joan is innocent—and it wasn't anything you could have done ... nothing anyone could have done to save Bill and Rachel. Even if you would have let Joan know about the puffer fish later that evening—Bill and Rachel were already dead. They had died within two hours after consuming that fish. Both Bill and Rachel were dead by the time Joan got home that night. Please don't blame yourself for their deaths."

Joan would've never murdered her parents!" Edith shrieked out. "She didn't feed her parents that fish; Albert and Mary did."

Edith was devastated and her entire body was trembling. Dr. Wilborn placed a chair next to Edith and then sat down beside her to comfort her. He placed his arm over her shoulders and said, "We're in shock just like you over the possibility that Albert and Mary may have poisoned

Bill and Rachel. Just breathe normally and relax. Just take your time and write out what you heard Albert and Mary say and everything will be okay."

Edith looked at Dr. Wilborn and said, "But my hands are shaking too much to write out another statement. Can I just tell you what happened again?"

"Sure you can. Deputy Goony will record your statement instead of you writing it down," Sheriff McClotin said.

Deputy Goony grabbed the digital voice recorder, set it down in front of Edith, and pushed the record button. Edith calmed down a bit and repeated what she had mentioned earlier about that dreadful day.

Edith finished her oral statement in eleven-minutes. Deputy Goony turned off the recorder, and Sheriff McClotin thanked her for her statement.

Edith just sat there in her chair, raised her head, and said, "How could Albert and Mary do such a thing? Why poison Bill and Rachel? They were great people, great parents, and great friends to me. Poor Joan ... she lost her parents needlessly."

"Edith, don't worry," Dr. Wilborn said. "We'll let Joan know what happened and tell her that you were a big help in solving the mystery of what happened to her parents."

"Deputy Goony, please take Edith home. She has provided us with all the information we need," Sheriff McClotin said.

"Sure," Deputy Goony replied.

Edith was visibly upset. She composed herself and said, "I didn't realize that Albert and Mary were poisoning Bill and Rachel. I would have come straight to you if I'd known that, Sheriff McClotin. I feel terrible."

"Now, now, Edith. It's not your fault they died. You had no idea what was going on," Sheriff McClotin said.

Edith couldn't control her emotions, and she started crying again as Deputy Goony escorted her out of the office to his cruiser to drive her home.

"The murder of Bill and Rachel may be solved with Edith's oral statement, which will clear Joan, but Joan's problems are not over with yet," Sheriff McClotin said. "Edith also provided a signed statement detailing what she witnessed Joan do with those duffel bags."

"I'm praying Joan will provide an explanation about those duffel bags," Dr. Wilborn said.

"Well, gentlemen, shall we drive up to Baltimore to present our autopsy report and witness statements to the Baltimore Police Department?" Detective Sanders asked.

"Yes," Sheriff McClotin somberly said.

Sheriff McClotin, Dr. Wilborn, and Detective Sanders gathered up their belongings and necessary paperwork and left for Baltimore.

34

Joan got out of her bed, went into her bathroom, looked into the mirror, and smiled. It was a bright and sunny Sunday morning—the morning following her surprise birthday party. She was happy and still beaming from the surprise birthday party that Jim had planned for her. She was truly shocked when she and Cindy had entered her condo and everyone shouted out *HAPPY BIRTHDAY!* It was Cindy's job to lure Joan away from her condo for a couple of hours while Jim and Robert prepared everything. All her coworkers from the bank were there, along with some of Jim's friends also. Joan enjoyed the ice cream cake, champagne, and all the various gifts presented to her.

Later that Saturday evening, after everyone had left, Joan thanked Jim for planning such a beautiful party and giving her the pink tennis shoes and pink jogging outfit as gifts. Before Jim left that Saturday evening ... he promised that he would return on Sunday afternoon and take her out to dinner. Joan kissed him, said good night, and watched him leave, get into his car, and drive off.

Joan continued to be jubilant that Sunday morning as she brushed her teeth and washed her face. But her euphoric mood immediately faded when she remembered she would have to make a decision that would change her life forever. This was the day that she intended to confront her lover and Jim with the news. She had made up her mind to tell them both whom she wanted to grow old with. She was tired of hiding her true feelings. The stress of it all was wearing on her, and she had to decide whom she wanted to spend the rest of her life with—today!

After having breakfast, Joan decided to drive to Jim's house first to tell him how she truly felt and whom she really wanted to be with. Before getting into her car, she noticed a silver Chevy Malibu parked across the street from her home with a man sitting inside. He was just staring at her. This man immediately turned his head and looked the other way when she made eye contact with him. She had never noticed that car in her neighborhood before, but it could've been one of her neighbors' friends or relatives visiting them. Before driving off, she glanced at this mysterious man once more, but he was talking on his cell phone and not paying any attention to her.

She soon forgot about the man in the Malibu and started to repeat what she had planned to say to Jim and her lover when she faced them. Joan had written down what she was going to say on a piece of paper while eating her breakfast that morning. It was important that she got it right.

She wanted to be truthful, sincere, and forthright with her statements to the both of them. At every red light on her way to Jim's house, she quickly perused her written statement to ensure she had it right.

Thirty-five-minutes later, Joan pulled up in front of Jim's house and parked. She knew Jim wasn't home because his car wasn't there. She used the next fifteen-minutes or so, while waiting for Jim to show up, to go over her written notes again. Fifteen-minutes later, she placed the sheet of paper on her lap and searched the street for Jim's car in both directions. Joan didn't see his car approaching from either direction, so she decided to leave. It was very unusual for Jim not to be home at ten o'clock on a Sunday morning. Just before she pulled off, she noticed that silver Malibu in her rearview mirror again. It was parked about twenty yards or so down the street behind her. She could see the driver talking on his cell phone again. Joan started to worry that this man could be stalking her. She cursed Jim for not being home when she really needed him because Jim would have figured out what to do.

Frustrated that Jim wasn't home, she drove off. While driving, she called her lover and decided to meet at their usual place. Joan explained to her lover that it was important to meet right now because she had something important to talk about. Her lover agreed and decided to meet Joan.

Joan smiled after hearing her lover's voice, but she was still quite nervous. She kept looking back in her rearview mirror for the silver Malibu, but she didn't see it.

Twenty-minutes later, Joan drove into the hotel parking area and parked. She searched the parking lot for that silver Malibu, but it wasn't there. She was a little bit on edge, so she hurried into the hotel. She searched the lobby, expecting to see the man who was driving the silver Malibu, but he wasn't there. Joan's lover had prepaid for their room, as usual, so Joan just picked up the room key from the front desk. She caught the elevator up to the fourth floor, entered the room, sat on the edge of the bed, and waited patiently for her lover to show up.

Ten-minutes later, the hotel room door opened. Joan leaped up from the bed, grabbed her lover and kissed her on the lips.

"I'm sorry I'm late," Cindy said after kissing Joan.

Cindy removed her coat, tossed it onto one of the hotel room chairs, and stretched out across the bed.

"When will you tell Robert that it's all over?" Joan said after sitting down on the bed next to Cindy.

"I plan on telling him today. And then I'm packing up my belongings and moving in with you," Cindy said.

"I wanted to tell Jim today, but he wasn't home," Joan said as she gently lay on top of Cindy. "Listen, all I ever wanted was you. The very first time I met you at the bank, I fell in love with you."

They kissed and then embraced as if they hadn't seen each other in months. Cindy gently pushed Joan's head away from hers and said, "Okay, you need to tell Jim today that you and I are a couple now. Tell him that I'm moving in and he needs to give you the extra set of house keys back."

Joan started to cry, laid down next to Cindy, held Cindy's hand and said, "I will tell him."

Cindy brushed Joan's hair back away from her brow and said, "Before we do anything, we must come clean with each other first. We deeply love each other, and nothing can change how we feel about each other—and I mean absolutely nothing! We must bring out all the skeletons in our closets now. If I'm going to commit to you for the rest of my life, I need to know everything about you, be it good or bad."

Joan looked a little surprised and caught off guard. She hadn't expected this from Cindy, but she realized Cindy was giving up her marriage to be with her.

"I realize what you'll be going through for me," Joan said. "You'll have to get a lawyer, divorce Robert, and leave your home. That is plenty of heartache, sorrow, and stress that you and Robert will have to deal with. I understand what you want from me, and I'm willing to tell you everything."

Cindy smiled, kissed Joan on her forehead, and said, "Please ... tell me everything. I want to know all about you ... no matter what it is. If we are to marry, you mustn't hide any secrets from me. I realize we both have done some devious things together, but we did those things together ... as a couple. I need to know what you may have done on your own in the past that may come back to haunt us."

As Joan lay on the bed facing Cindy ... she couldn't help but to think about that deceitful thing they did together just to be together : *Cindy and Joan had asked Kim if they could use her home as a cover while they made out at Joan's condominium. At first Kim didn't want to go along with their plan, because she thought it was immoral, but after a few minutes of Joan and Cindy begging her to help them, Kim agreed. Kim carried out their plans perfectly. Kim answered her home phone when Robert called and told him that Cindy couldn't talk because she was using the bathroom, but she would let Cindy know that he called when she got out of the bathroom. All the while, Kim made Robert believe that Cindy was actually at her house, but Cindy was actually with Joan at Joan's house.*

Joan quickly snapped out of her reverie and said, "You're so right. All the lies end today. I don't blame you for wanting to know what's going on in my life. You probably were confused when I asked you to pretend to be Mary. At first, I didn't think you would do it, but you did. You loved me so much that you actually disguised your voice and pretended to be Mary. I thought of that crazy idea when I was in my kitchen, drinking my sorrows away. That's when I decided to call you from my kitchen, because Jim was sitting right there in my living room, watching TV. I didn't want him to hear our conversation, so I had to speak quietly. After I convinced you to be Mary, I went into the living room and pretended to dial Mary's phone number, but it was actually your phone number. Jim thought he was actually talking to Mary. He was convinced. You should have seen the smile on Jim's face. Thank you for following my instructions, to the letter, on what to say to him; I really appreciated that."

"I don't have any regrets for what I did, but I'm still confused as to why I even had to pretend to be Mary when the real Mary could have talked to Jim. It all just doesn't make any sense to me," Cindy said.

Joan didn't respond. She just looked at Cindy and started to cry. Joan was feeling guilty about all the devious things she had forced Cindy to do just to conceal her lies. Cindy waited for a response, but Joan was mum. Cindy continued by saying, "You didn't know this, but when I pretended to be Mary, Jim had asked me if Albert and I could come to Baltimore for your surprise birthday party."

"Wow ... I didn't know that. That was sweet of Jim to try to invite them, but I didn't love Jim anymore. I was in love with you."

"You know that I love you too. Now, what's all this secrecy surrounding Albert and Mary?"

Joan paused, sighed, and then said, "I'm going to tell you the truth about them now. But before I start ... I must ask you something first."

"Sure, go ahead," Cindy said.

With a bit of apprehension, Joan said, "My heart is still hurting about an incident that happened about a week ago. I was enraged when I first saw you with this person, but then I thought you would eventually explain it to me."

Cindy looked confused. She sat up in the bed and said, "Whatever you saw, I can explain. I'm not hiding anything. I love you too much to jeopardize our relationship."

"Okay. When I drove by your house, one day, last week, I saw you hug some guy. After you hugged him, he drove off and you went into your house. At first, I didn't know what to think. But then I felt a little jealous of him. I quickly became upset about it, and I wanted to find out what was going on. I knew you would have a good explanation about the whole ordeal once I asked you. So, I'm asking you now ... who was that guy you hugged?"

Cindy smiled and said, "I can explain. While Robert was at work that day, my car broke down. I came out of Food Lion after grocery shopping, and my car wouldn't start. I called Robert, and he sent one of their courtesy drivers, Reginald, out to pick me up and take me home. Reginald is the guy who's assigned to drive people home or to work after they drop off their cars for repairs or certain maintenance. He also picks them up at their place of business or home when their cars are ready. I've known Reginald for years. When Reginald dropped me off, I gave him a hug and thanked him. Reginald is like a brother to me. Nothing's going on between the two of us. By the way, it was a bad battery. Robert purchased another one that day and installed it. My car is running perfectly now."

Joan smiled, sat up, moved close to Cindy, and said, "I knew it wasn't anything to worry about."

Cindy hugged Joan and said, "Now that we settled that ... what's going on with Albert and Mary? I still don't understand why you wanted me to pretend to be Mary."

Joan faltered for a moment, took in a deep breath, and exhaled. She looked Cindy in her eyes and said, "I wanted Jim to believe that Albert and Mary existed and really lived in Fall City. The only way to prove that was to have you pretend to be Mary and talk to him. Remember when I told you that Albert and Mary had moved to Baltimore with me from Fall City, but then they moved back to Fall City after only living in Baltimore for a couple of months?"

"Yes."

"Well, they never moved here with me. They never left Fall City."

Cindy looked puzzled for a moment and said, "Why say Albert and Mary moved here with you when they didn't? If they never moved from Fall City, then why did you need me to pretend to be Mary?"

Joan stood up, paced back and forth for a few seconds around the hotel room, and then took a seat in the sofa chair next to the bed. She looked down toward the floor and said, "Let me start from the beginning. I've told you many times about Dr. Wilborn, Sheriff McClotin, and others in my hometown of Fall City. They were all like family to me, and they treated me great. But I never told you about the time Dr. Wilborn asked me to come to his office one afternoon because he had something to discuss with me. That day Dr. Wilborn told me about the conversation he had with Albert and Mary about my peculiar behavior. After hearing the disgusting stories about me, which were told by Albert and Mary to Dr. Wilborn, I became livid. Albert and Mary told Dr. Wilborn I was hallucinating. They said I was talking very loudly at night to God! They said that I was burning my parents' pictures and other items belonging to them. They even said that I was abducted by aliens."

With a disturbed look, Cindy said, "That's horrible!"

"But, Dr. Wilborn ensured me that Albert and Mary loved me and was only worried about my well-being ... and that they wanted him to help me. Dr. Wilborn concluded that the Zoloft I was taking was the root cause of my problems. So, before I left Dr. Wilborn's office, we came to an agreement that I would stop taking my Zoloft. After talking to Dr. Wilborn that day, I went home and acted like I always did around Albert and Mary. I acted as if everything was normal and nothing was wrong. I'd stopped taking the Zoloft, and I continued to treat Albert and Mary as my loving family, but I had a feeling that the Zoloft never really caused me to have those issues. For some reason, and I don't know why, I thought that Albert and Mary had made all of those accusations up. I had made up my mind to find out the truth. I started snooping around the house one evening and discovered the ugly truth. I walked by Albert and Mary's bedroom late one night, and I overheard them talking about how they had lied to Dr. Wilborn about me. Everything they'd told Dr. Wilborn was a lie; they'd made it all up. They wanted it to look as if I was going crazy. They wanted Dr. Wilborn to believe that I murdered my parents. Albert and Mary, over the years, had stolen pictures, picture frames, a gold locket, and many other valuable items that belonged to me. That's why I couldn't find my parents' pictures and other valuable items—because they had stolen them. That night, I put my ear close to Albert and Mary's bedroom door and heard them discussing money. They talked about the large sum of money they'd received from the insurance company for my parents' deaths. And, how they were planning to travel to Las Vegas with that money."

Joan paused for a moment, raised her head up, and wiped a tear from her face just as Cindy said, "Albert and Mary are despicable."

Joan frowned and said, "Albert and Mary had planned to go to Vegas and party for an entire week. They thought I was asleep, but I had my ear pressed up against their bedroom door, listening to every word they said. I heard them discuss how they were planning to withdraw additional money from my parents' estate and put it into a savings account for themselves. Since they were the trustees of the estate for my parents, they had access to everything. They wanted Dr. Wilborn and other people to believe that I was going crazy so they could inherit my parent's estate. The next thing I heard made me sick. They actually bragged about how they had used certain parts of my puffer fish to poison my parents. I was filled with rage, disbelief, and the feeling of being helpless. I started crying, but I made sure they didn't hear me. I wanted to call the sheriff to let him know what really happened to my parents, but I never did. I wiped the tears from my face and almost opened their door to confront them, but somehow I controlled my anger. I didn't realize that they hated my parents so much that they killed them ... for money. They were pure evil; they were devils in disguise."

There was dead silence for a moment. Cindy stood up from the bed, knelt down in front of Joan, and looked into her eyes. Joan had dark circles underneath her eyes, her face was pale, and she looked incurably sad. Cindy's face was twisted in anguish as tears ran down her face.

Cindy kissed Joan on her lips and said, "My heart aches so much for you. How could you have tolerated living with them after hearing that? Albert and Mary were monsters. You had to have been distraught to hear them say that. You should have let the sheriff know that Albert and Mary murdered your parents."

"I should have, but I didn't let the sheriff or

anyone else know that Albert and Mary were murderers. I almost threw up at the foot of their bedroom door when they said they had fed two of my puffer fish to my parents for dinner that fateful day. That made my blood boil. That's when I decided to murder them."

Cindy took in a deep breath, stopped crying, stood up, and sat down on the edge of the bed, facing Joan. Cindy's eyes were bloodshot from all her crying, and she was trembling from the fear of what she thought she might hear next.

Cindy looked at Joan and said, "No matter what happened—I will always love you."

Joan started to tremble but continued with her story. "Albert, Mary, and I had intended on moving to Baltimore after I graduated from college. My plan was to murder them as soon as I graduated, but I had to wait until the night before I left for Baltimore before killing them. Albert and Mary didn't know what hit them. The night I murdered them, they were all excited about moving to Baltimore. They were packing their suitcases and other personal items when I killed them—but not before I tortured them. Those two deserved every bit of pain I imposed upon them. No one in Fall City would ever know that I stuffed their lifeless bodies into separate duffel bags and dumped them into the lake. After dumping their worthless carcasses, I drove to Baltimore. All of Fall City thought they'd traveled to Baltimore with me. Moving to Baltimore was my perfect alibi. No one would miss them, ask about them, or come looking for them, because they were supposed to have been with me in Baltimore. And, if anyone did want to get in touch with them, I had a plan. My plan was to say that they had become homesick and moved right back to Fall City not long after moving to Baltimore with me. I would even embellish my story by saying that I drove them to the Baltimore Greyhound Bus Station, where they boarded a bus for home. That would clear me of having anything to do with Albert's and Mary's disappearances. I really tricked Albert and Mary on the night I murdered them ... just like they tricked my parents. I mixed ten sleeping pills and four Vicodin into each of their glasses of wine. I convinced them to have a glass of wine with me in celebration of my graduation and us moving to Baltimore. Thirty-minutes after they drank their wine, they were completely passed out. That's when I went to work. I dragged them both into the bathroom and placed them, one at a time, into the bathtub, where I pulled out all their teeth, cut off the tips of each of their fingers, and cut off their legs. I burned all of their identification along with their fingertips and teeth. I couldn't take the chance of them ever being identified if they were found."

Cindy almost fainted as she watched and listened with numbed dismay. She felt nauseated, and her head was spinning around in circles. To prevent herself from falling over, she gripped the edge of the bed and held on tight. Her breath quickened, and she gasped for air. A chill ran up her spine. She couldn't believe what she was hearing. She couldn't cry anymore because she was in shock. She started to breathe normally again, regained her composure, and tried to speak—but she couldn't.

"It wasn't easy pulling, cutting, and hacking on Albert and Mary, because every now and then they would shriek out in pain—especially when I started pulling their teeth. At first their eyes would open up and they would moan out loud. And then they would close their eyes again. When I started cutting into their legs, they damn near jumped out of the bathtub. I don't know how they reacted like that because they were still out cold. They were like zombies ... alive, but dead! The drugs and wine that I'd given them really did the trick. All in all ... it was a bizarre evening. After all their blood had drained into the bathtub, I placed each body into its own personal duffel bag. But I had a problem. When I tried to stick their severed legs into the duffel bags with the bodies, their shoes were getting in the way. So, I removed their shoes. After neatly fitting the legs in, I just closed up the duffel bags and put a lock on each to keep them secured. The next morning, I dumped those duffel bags into the lake before I left for Baltimore. Now you know why I couldn't let Jim talk to Albert or Mary. They were dead. Thanks to you for pretending to be Mary ... Jim really believed that I was still in contact with them.

Cindy didn't know what to say or do. She just sat on the edge of the bed without moving a muscle.

Joan finally mustered up some strength, stood

up from her chair, and walked over to Cindy. She hugged her and said, "I hope you still love me."

Cindy didn't say a word. She quickly scooted off the edge of the bed and walked toward the door. Joan followed Cindy and grabbed her arm just as she took hold of the doorknob and slowly opened the door. Before Joan could say another word, Detective Sanders, Detective Russo, Sheriff McClotin, and Dr. Wilborn walked in. Joan didn't know what was going on. Detective Russo was a homicide detective for the Baltimore City Police. He was the person in the Silver Malibu who had been following her.

"Joan Witherspoon, you're under arrest for the murder of Albert and Mary Niphon," Detective Russo said.

Detective Sanders spun Joan around, placed her hands behind her back, and handcuffed her.

Joan had a look of desperation and confusion on her face as she sadly looked at Dr. Wilborn, the sheriff, and the love of her life—Cindy. Cindy held her head down and turned away from Joan.

"What is going on? Cindy ... Cindy, what's happening?" Joan asked as tears poured down her face.

Dr. Wilborn and Sheriff McClotin were at a loss for words. They could only watch helplessly as Detective Russo read Joan her Miranda rights. "You have the right to remain silent. Anything you say can and will be used against you in a court of law. You have the right to speak to an attorney and to have an attorney present during any questioning. If you cannot afford a lawyer, one will be provided for you at government expense. Do you understand what I just said?"

"I don't understand what you're saying. Why are you arresting me? Cindy, what's going on?" Joan cried out.

Cindy finally turned, faced Joan, and said, "I'm so sorry. The police told me that you probably murdered Albert and Mary, and they needed me to get you to confess to their murders. It all happened when Sheriff McClotin and Dr. Wilborn came by your condo with the intentions of talking to you but you weren't home. I was there because you'd asked me to look after your puffer fish that day while you and Jim had lunch together. The police had your place under surveillance for a few days, and that's when they discovered that you and I had rendezvoused at this hotel a few times. After explaining that they knew what was going on between you and me, they asked if I could help them solve a murder case. This murder case involved Albert and Mary Niphon and you. I was reluctant to work with the police at first, but I changed my mind because I wanted to prove that you didn't murder Albert and Mary Niphon. So, I agreed to wear a listening device during our conversation. I just knew that you didn't murder them, but I was wrong. In a way, part of me can't blame you for what you did, and part of me can't believe that you murdered them. This is heartbreaking. Now that they have heard your story, you won't be charged with the death of your parents."

Joan leaned forward to kiss Cindy, but

Detective Russo pushed her toward the door and out into the hotel hallway. Cindy, Dr. Wilborn, and Sheriff McClotin were all bewildered, hurt, and in shock. But most of all they felt deceived as Detectives Sanders and Russo escorted Joan through the hallway, out of the hotel, and into the waiting police car.

The End